Goosebumps

EAT CHEESE AND BARF!

R. U. SLIME

An Unauthorized Parody

Not a Goosebumps Book

Bullseye Books

Random House New York

An Unauthorized Parody

Not a Goosebumps Book

A BULLSEYE BOOK PUBLISHED BY RANDOM HOUSE, INC.

Copyright © 1995 by Robert Hughes. All rights reserved under
International and Pan-American Copyright Conventions.
Published in the United States by Random House, Inc., New York,
and simultaneously in Canada by Random House of Canada
Limited, Toronto.

Library of Congress Catalog Card Number: 95-070043
ISBN: 0-679-87935-8
RL: 4.01

Manufactured in the United States of America
10 9 8 7 6 5 4 3 2 1

CHAPTER 1

"Drink your milk, Billy, it's good for you," my mom said, smiling.

I couldn't believe what I was hearing. Drink my milk?

"But, Mom, you know what happens if I drink milk—"

"Don't argue with your mother, Billy, drink your milk," Dad said. He looked over his bifocals and winked at me.

"But I'll barf!" I said, holding my nose and sucking in my breath. I have some kind of weird enzyme in my stomach. It's pretty rare. All I need to do is get a whiff of milk and—chunks city!

"Gross! Mom, Billy said 'barf' at the table!" Jennifer made a face at me. I didn't know what was worse—looking at the milk or at my sister's zits.

"I heard him, dear. Thank you, but you don't have to say it again. Now, Billy, I want you to have a big glass of milk. It's good for you, sweetheart."

"But, Mom—"

"Drink it!" my parents both said at the same time. I reached out for the milk carton. My hand trembled. I drew the carton toward me across the table. My stomach was already doing flipflops. Jennifer started laughing. She has the dumbest laugh in the world.

"Drink your milk, Billy. Drink it all up!" Jennifer sang, scrunching up her nose. She looked even uglier than usual—believe it or not.

"Shut up, pizza-face!" I said finally. When I call her that, she goes crazy. She starts screaming, then runs to her room. But this time, she just kept staring at me and cackling.

I started sweating as I reached for the glass. As if my hand had a life of its own. Sweat trickled down my arms under my R.E.M. T-shirt.

"You're not getting up from this table until that glass is empty, young man," my dad said.

I couldn't believe they were going to make me do it. My mom made drink-up motions with her hand. The glass touched my lips. I could smell it now. A horrible, sickly sweet smell. My stomach churned.

I tilted the glass up. I begged them with my eyes—*don't make me do this!* My glasses fogged up. I poured the milk down my throat and swallowed every last drop.

I shut my eyes tight and waited. Nothing.

Then I felt it—the revenge of the enzyme!

I barfed! All over the table—meatloaf, I think. I spewed all over my sister until she was dripping with chunks. I couldn't control it. I barfed on my dad and ruined the paper he was reading. Then the biggest barf of all started coming up. I turned toward my mom. Not my mom! I could feel the slimy stuff coming up my throat. I tried to fight it—no use!

My mom screamed, "No, Billy, no, Billy, *Billeeeee!*"

CHAPTER 2

"Billy, Billy, wake up," Mom said gently.

A dream. It was just a goofy dream. I had crusted drool on my chin, but no barf. My mom was looking back at me from the front seat of our station wagon. Jennifer was sitting next to me. She had her Walkman on. She scowled at me, showing off her new braces—business as usual.

If that had been a dream, maybe this trip was a dream too. I could only hope.

Then my mom pointed out the window. "Look, honey, here we are."

I looked where she was pointing:

INTERNATIONAL MILK PRODUCTS
WELCOMES YOU TO BLEDSOE, NEW YORK
THE COTTAGE CHEESE CAPITAL OF THE WORLD

My mom read the sign aloud. It was shaped like a cow and glowed in the dark.

We really were moving to the cottage cheese capital of the world. Great. We really had left behind my friends, my school, and the treehouse that I built with Tommy Dillard when we were eight.

"What do you think, Billy?" Dad asked. "You're pretty excited, I'll bet."

"Oh, yeah, real excited," I said. Milk Town, USA. My stomach was churning already.

"What's International Milk Products?" Jennifer asked, slipping off her earphones.

"It's one of the biggest dairy products manu-facturers in the state, maybe on the whole East Coast," Dad told her. He gets excited about things like that.

"Their biggest plant is right here in Bledsoe," he added. "Great-Grandpa Theo used to work for them."

"I think everyone in Bledsoe works for them," Mom put in.

"Maybe you could talk to them about a job in their public relations department," Dad told her. My mom works in advertising and stuff like that.

"Whoever came up with 'Cottage Cheese Capital of the World' could use a little help, that's for sure," she said.

5

"Yeah, that's gross," Jennifer said. "Who wants to live in the cottage cheese capital of the world?"

"Yeah, Mom, why don't we turn around now and go home?" I suggested. "We could think of this moving idea as a dark chapter in our family history that no one ever talks about."

No answer—just an annoying smile from my mom.

We stopped at a red light. I was desperate. "Please, Mom, please, Dad, let's go back to Syracuse. I'm sure even Jennifer thinks this move is a big mistake." But my sister was bopping to the Pimples or whatever stupid band she was listening to. The light turned green and we drove into town. There was only one thing left for me to do.

"Oh, please, please, please, please, please, Mom, please, Dad, let's not move here. Let's go home!"

My mom turned around. She wasn't smiling anymore. "Stop it, Billy. You're too old to whine. Now just sit back and be still."

"Anyway, buddy," my dad said, "we *are* home—as soon as we find the farm. I haven't been here since I was Billy's age, you know. I don't remember where we turn off Main to get to the farm."

My dad had inherited Breakwind Farms from my great-grandpa Theo Fudder. If it wasn't for stupid Breakwind Farms, we wouldn't be moving. I hated it already.

While Dad looked for the turnoff, I checked out Main Street. We were right in the middle of downtown Bledsoe. Everything was closed. We passed a bank and a gas station and a sign that flashed MOO 'N' DOO. Whatever that meant.

"Hey, dork," Jennifer said, tapping me on the shoulder. "There's a place especially for you."

I looked out the window. It was a big old building, kind of like an old-fashioned bank. A sign above the door read IMP MILK MUSEUM. I couldn't believe it. A whole museum devoted to the thing I hated most in the world!

"That's it, Curdle Street," Dad announced, turning left.

"Ooooh, what's that smell?" Jennifer asked, holding her nose.

Then I smelled it. Cows. Lots and lots of cows.

My dad took a deep breath, as if he was really into it. "That is the smell of what made this town great, sweetheart."

"Cow doo?" Jennifer asked.

My mom turned around again. This time she was smiling. "Jennifer!"

I decided to give it one last try. "Please, you guys. I hate this town. It stinks, and it's ugly!"

Mom messed my hair up. "I'll admit that it's not the best smell, but we'll get used to it. And I think the town is cute." She turned to my dad. "Don't you think so, sweetheart?"

"I have nothing but good memories of Bledsoe. I love this town. And I'm sure you kids will, too, if you give it a chance."

We left town on Curdle Street and then turned onto a dirt road. The only lights were the headlights of our station wagon as we lurched and bumped along the gravel. And suddenly, there it was—Breakwind.

"No way. This *cannot* be it," Jennifer announced, popping her gum.

"Well this *is* it," Mom said. Even she sounded nervous. "Right, honey?"

"Just like I remember it," Dad said. "C'mon, gang, let's go exploring."

Mom and Dad got out. Jennifer and I stayed where we were—stuck to the seat. We stared at the big old house. It was falling apart. The porch sagged on one side. The screen door flapped in the breeze, which was blowing the cow smell into the car.

Dad banged on the roof of the car. "C'mon, you guys. Hey, Billy, hand me that flashlight

8

from the glove compartment, would you?"

That broke the spell. Jennifer showed me her braces. "Welcome home, dork-brain."

"Thanks a lot, tinsel-teeth," I shot back at her. I grabbed the flashlight and took it to Dad.

"Looks kind of run-down," he admitted, shining the light on the house.

Mom clapped her hands together. "Nothing a little elbow grease can't fix," she said, walking toward the house.

"*Daaaaad!*" Jennifer came running around the car and grabbed Dad's arm. "Dad, Dad, there's something out there!"

"What, honey, what's out there? Where?"

"Over there. I heard something!"

Then we heard it too. We all gathered around Dad. He swung the flashlight over to where Jennifer was pointing. There was nothing there. And then a ghostly white shape appeared.

"*Aaaaahhhhhhhhh!*" Jennifer screamed.

Dad laughed. "It's just a cow, sweetie," he told my sister.

Mom said, "What's that in its mouth?"

We all looked a little closer. The cow had something hanging out of its mouth—a human arm!

CHAPTER
3

"Run for the hills—it's a man-eating cow!" I shouted.

Dad dove back into the station wagon and grabbed the tire iron from under the front seat. Jennifer hid behind my mom. I was frozen to the spot.

"Stand back, everybody!" Dad commanded, taking a few steps toward the carnivorous cow.

"Careful, sweetheart," my mom whispered.

And then a man came around the corner. A skinny dude with long black hair. He was wearing a tuxedo.

"Hello," he said, patting the strange cow on the rump. Then he took the arm. He walked toward us, a big smile on his face. "You must be the Fudders. I've been expecting you."

"Yes, we are," Dad said. "And who might you be?"

"I'm Armand, the caretaker."

"What about that cow—and the arm?" Jennifer cried, still hiding behind Mom.

"That's Martha," Armand explained. "She's the oldest cow on the property—your great-grandfather's favorite. And the arm is mine. Don't mind Martha—she likes to play games sometimes."

I saw that one of Armand's tuxedo sleeves was dangling loose. He slid the arm up the sleeve. There was a clicking sound, and then Armand smiled. "Don't tell me Mr. Fudder didn't tell you about me," he said.

"He did mention something once about hiring some hands to help him out," Mom said, staring at Armand's artificial arm.

"Well, he only hired one, and that's me," Armand said. "You folks go on in now. There's some coffee on the stove. The light switch is right by the door."

I couldn't take my eyes off the guy's fake arm. It was the coolest thing I had ever seen. I wondered if it was bionic.

"Can I touch your arm?" I asked.

My mother gasped. "Billy, that's not polite."

"Oh, that's okay. Sure, you can touch it. But be careful—sometimes I think this old arm has a mind of its own." He swung his arm up level with my face. The shiny plastic felt cold and

11

smooth.

"Cool," I said. I took a step forward to get a better look and—*splat!* I'd stepped right smack in the middle of a cow pie. And I had on my brand-new boots, too.

"Oh, Billy," Mom groaned.

"Gross!" Jennifer exclaimed.

"All right, everybody inside," Dad ordered. "Billy, you make sure you get all that stuff off your boots before you take one step in the house."

Mom and Dad and Jennifer went in. I bent over to try and clean my boots. Armand knelt down beside me. "If you think my arm is cool," he whispered in my ear, "wait till I show you all the tricks I can do with it."

I smiled at him. He seemed kind of weird, but nice.

"Maybe I'll tell you how I lost the real one sometime," he continued.

"How did you lose it?" I was hoping it would be a really gross story.

Armand looked at me and made a whooshing sound. "Milking machine. Sucked it clean off." Then he started laughing.

The lights went on in the house. I found a stick and started scraping the gunk off my boots. When I looked up again, Armand was gone. But

Martha, the cow, was still there—staring at me as if she was a person or something.

After I finished cleaning my boots, I went in. Inside, the house was a disaster. All the furniture was covered with sheets, like in a haunted house. In the living room was a big fireplace. And over the fireplace hung a portrait of my great-grandfather. He was standing in the middle of a big field with a cow. He didn't look like a dairy farmer. He looked more like some kind of scientist. He had on a white coat with one of those plastic protectors in the top pocket.

Dad came into the living room and stood next to me.

"I thought Great-Grandpa Theo was a farmer," I said. "He sure doesn't look like one."

"Well, he wasn't an ordinary farmer," Dad explained. "He was also a research scientist."

"What did he research?"

"Ways to make young guys like you stronger and healthier," Dad said, chuckling.

"With milk?" I guessed, with a sinking feeling.

"Yes, with milk, Billy-boy. Everybody loves milk except you. And I think that's going to be a problem for us here."

"It is?" I asked.

Dad nodded. "So we've decided to send you to live with your aunt Gladys in Iowa."

I couldn't believe what I was hearing. Aunt Gladys was about a hundred years old. And Bledsoe didn't look so hot, but I didn't want to move to the middle of nowhere—2,000 miles from my folks.

"Are you serious, Dad?" I gulped.

"No," he replied, then slapped his knee and burst out laughing. What a kidder!

"But seriously, son, I know it's going to be a little difficult for you here at first. You'll probably be miserable and lonely, but you'll get over it. It'll be an adventure, an exciting one! Right?"

"Right," I said weakly.

"That's my boy." Dad ran his fingers through his hair, but that just made it messier. My hair is like his—black and bushy and wiry.

Mom and Jennifer came into the living room. Mom was wiping her hands on a dishrag. "What are you fellas talking about out here?"

Jennifer lifted a sheet off a chair. She frowned and let the sheet fall. A huge cloud of dust rose. Jennifer started coughing—and then crying.

My mom ran over to her. "Jennifer, what's the matter, honey?" she asked gently.

Suddenly, my sister screamed. She beat on the back of the chair—raising more and more dust.

"I hate this place!" she wailed. "How could

14

you do this? How could you make me leave all my friends to come *here*?"

"Honey, please, calm down," Mom said.

I knew exactly what was coming next. She didn't care about her old school or her friends. She only cared about one thing—

"Scotty!" she cried. "How could you make me leave Scotty?"

Scotty Roberts is—was—her boyfriend back home. Dad looked at me and kind of smiled.

"Scotty was going to ask me to go to the prom and now my life is completely ruined!"

The screen door burst open, and Armand trudged in with a suitcase under each arm. He grinned and dropped the suitcases. He walked up to my sister. "Hey now, missy, what's the trouble here? Is somebody missing somebody, is that what I hear?"

"Yes, they"—she pointed at my parents— "made me leave my boyfriend!"

"Well, don't you worry about a thing. Why do you think I'm wearing this tuxedo tonight?"

"Because you're a weirdo," Jennifer responded. I had to admit it was a good answer.

"All right, young lady, that's enough—" Dad began.

"That's all right, she's upset," Armand said. "It's hard to be separated from people you love. But what if I told you I dug this old monkey suit

15

out to see if it still fit, so I could wear it to the big dance next week?"

"Big dance?" Jennifer asked, wiping her eyes.

"That's right, the biggest event of the year. The Dairy Dance! IMP sponsors it every year. That's where they crown the Dairy Queen. And there's lots of food and fun and dancing until— well, until the cows come home."

Dad laughed. I didn't get it.

"Actually, we usually get home before the cows, because they spend the night," Armand explained.

"There are really cows there?" I asked him. I was getting sick just thinking about all this dairy stuff.

"Sure—what would this town be like without 'em? There wouldn't be a town at all, that's what." He turned back to Jennifer. "You know who else will be there?"

"Who?"

"All the most eligible young bachelors in town, just waiting to meet the pretty new girl over at Breakwind. Why, you'll have to beat them off with a stick!"

"You think so?" Jennifer asked.

"I know so." Armand winked at her.

Jennifer seemed to think for a minute. Then she grabbed Mom by the arm. "Oh, Mom, c'mon. You have to help me pick out something to wear!"

"But, honey, there's plenty of time."

Jennifer kept at it, though, and ended up dragging Mom upstairs.

Girls are so weird.

"I bet you left a whole string of crying girls behind, huh, Billy?" Armand asked.

"I don't think so."

"What about that little girlfriend of yours, Ginny Kapimpski?" Dad asked.

"Ginny *Stravinsky* is not my girlfriend," I informed them. We had the same English class and we both liked White Ninja movies, but that was it. When I told her I was moving, she punched me in the stomach as hard as she could.

"You're right to think that way, Billy," Armand said. "Girls are nothing but trouble. And I expect you'll have a heap of trouble, come the Dairy Dance."

"Dad, I'm kind of tired," I said.

Dad stopped laughing and looked at his watch. "Gosh, I didn't realize how late it was. Why don't we go upstairs and stake you a claim on a room. Gotta make sure you don't take the biggest one for yourself!"

CHAPTER
4

I ended up with a big room in the front of the house, in spite of Dad's joke. It had a sloping ceiling with windows kind of cut into it. My dad called them dormer windows. The best part was that it was all the way down the hall from Jennifer's room.

Mom gave me some clean sheets out of a trunk. I climbed into bed and stared up at the stars. I was tired, but I couldn't sleep. I was kind of excited, I guess. And nervous. It was summer vacation and I didn't know anyone.

I opened the window to get some air. I took a deep breath, but the air smelled like cow doo. This was going to be my worst summer ever.

Looking down, I saw Armand come out of the house. I was about to say hi or something when that weird cow walked up behind him. The cow nudged him in the back and Armand turned around.

"No," Armand said, "it's not necessary."

The cow just looked at him. For a second, I thought I saw its mouth move. But it must only have been chewing. I thought Armand was weird, but arguing with a cow?

"If I couldn't find it in all this time, what makes you think they will?" Armand asked.

Find what? What was he talking about?

Suddenly the cow swung her head around and looked right at me. Her eyes glowed in the light coming from the living-room window. Armand looked up too.

I ducked.

The light was off in my room.

Had he seen me?

"Billy Fudder, what are you doing up there?"

I didn't know what to do.

"I know you're up there," he called up to me.

I peered over the windowsill. They were still there, staring at me.

"Hi," I said, trying to sound normal.

Armand was silent a moment longer. I think he glanced at the cow again. "What are you doing up there, spying on people?"

"I wasn't spying. I was just getting some fresh air."

"That's good. Because it's not nice to spy on people."

"Well, good night," I said. "I'm pretty tired. I'm going to bed."

"Good night, Billy. Sleep tight." He stepped forward into a pile of cow doo. He looked down at the mess on his shoe and then looked back at me. "I'll see you in the morning." He waved up at me, and suddenly his fake arm came off and flew across the yard! It really did seem to have a life of its own. I wondered if I could get him to fling it at Jennifer.

"Billy, hey, Billy, you little runt! Get up!"

I opened my eyes. I was in my new room with the slanty ceiling. The sun was pouring through the windows. I could hear birds singing. And the air smelled like cows.

"Get up, it's time for breakfast!" Jennifer was pounding on the door. Oh, no, not breakfast—unless Armand was cooking.

"I'm getting up, brace-face." I heard her going down the stairs.

I put some running pants on and went to take a shower. The bathroom was kind of cool-looking and old-fashioned. You flushed the toilet by pulling a chain. The bathtub had claw feet. I padded across the freezing checkerboard floor and glanced at the mirror.

I had zits all over my face!

CHAPTER 5

"Aaaaaaahhhhhh!"

I touched the mirror.

They weren't zits on *my* face. Jennifer had been squeezing her pimples on the mirror.

I turned on the hot water. It burned my hand like fire as I washed the zit pus away. I thought I was going to barf. Man, teenagers are so gross!

I poured some rubbing alcohol that I had found under the sink on my hand. I stayed in the shower for a half hour. Dad came up twice to see if I was okay and to let me know breakfast was getting cold.

When I finally felt clean again, I got out of the shower and got dressed. What a way to start a summer vacation!

It hit me all over again—summer vacation with no friends and nothing to do. At least Jennifer was going to be busy thinking about the stupid Dairy Dance. She wouldn't have too much time to torture me.

"Good morning, Billy!" Dad greeted me from the kitchen table. He had on a checkered shirt and jeans and boots. I think that was the first time I ever saw my dad in jeans. He's a business guy. He makes a lot of money selling aquarium accessories, like bubbling divers and treasure chests that open and close by themselves. I guess he figured he was going to be a farmer now.

"We thought you fell down the drain," he said, laughing.

"Jennifer was popping her zits on the mirror again," I said.

"I was not. I don't have any zits, do I, Mom?"

Mom was at the stove. She was dressed kind of like a farmer too—in an old-fashioned dress with blue and red stripes and long sleeves.

What was she doing at the stove?

She turned to Jennifer. "Well, sweetheart, have you been using that scrub I gave you?"

Jennifer's face bunched up like a fist. It got all knobby and creased. "Daddy, I don't have zits, do I?"

Dad looked at Mom and shrugged. "No, sweetheart. Your skin is as fresh as a little peach."

22

And just as fuzzy, I thought.

Dad pinched her cheek. Sick—how could he touch that pizza skin?

"Are you cooking, Mom?" I asked.

"Yes, I thought it would be nice for us all to have a good, hearty country breakfast. Are you hungry?"

"Not really," I lied.

"Well, you have to eat something. Breakfast is the most important meal of the day, you know!"

I smiled.

Mom picked something off the stove and walked toward me. It had a terrible smell. She put a plate down in front of me. There was something black and squishy on it.

What was it?

What was my mom trying to feed me?

CHAPTER 6

"It's pancakes!" she announced.

I love my mom and all. She's a really good mom. Once, when I was a kid, she stood in the rain all day to watch me play soccer. But she can't cook!

"Pancakes?"

"Yes, your favorite," she said. "Go ahead, dig in!"

They were really gross-looking. They were black on both sides. I stuck my fork in them and some uncooked batter oozed out, like the pus on the mirror.

I looked at Dad. He understood my dilemma, but there was nothing he could do.

"I'm really not that hungry, Mom. Maybe I'll just have some toast."

"But you have to eat something," she insisted.

Dad saved the day. "He's probably got a nervous stomach. You know, with the move and everything. Just have some juice and toast, Billy, and then get outside and have fun!" It was a good excuse. Everybody knew my stomach was weird anyway.

Mom looked doubtful, but she gave me some partially burned toast. Jennifer grabbed my plate and started eating the pancakes. "I'll take them if you don't want them," she said with her mouth full. "They're great!"

It was about two miles from Breakwind to town. I passed the barn on the way out and saw Armand puttering around with some machines that looked like pumps. I waved at him, and he waved back with his fake arm. I was half hoping it would fly off. I wondered if he could get it to come back to him, like a boomerang.

I went out the gate. The pastures spread out, all green and smooth. There were a lot of cows dotting the rich grass, chewing and walking and walking and chewing. Okay, so cows aren't the most exciting animals in the world. At least I was getting used to the cow smell—just as Mom said I would.

After a while, I noticed a sign on one side of the road. There was a picture of a really creepy-looking old guy on it. He was smiling, but it didn't look as if he got much practice. He had a big pointy nose and little eyes and some kind of weird stain all over his bald head. His long, scrawny neck was all wrinkled and gross. He was wearing a lab coat and waving one finger. The sign read:

JONATHAN CURDLE SEZ:
KEEP BLEDSOE BEAUTIFUL—DON'T LITTER!
THIS MESSAGE IS BROUGHT TO YOU BY YOUR
FRIENDS AT IMP.

I was looking at the sign when I heard a giant bee. Or maybe it was a swarm of bees. I looked around to see where it was coming from and saw a cloud of dust coming up the road, heading straight toward me. The buzzing got louder and louder. I was about to run when I realized what it was...one of those super-cool motor scooters!

The guy on the scooter had on a helmet and gloves. I moved over to the side of the road to let him pass, thinking how cool it would be to have one of those things. *Splat!* Another cow pie!

I scraped my shoe against the fencepost. The scooter stopped. The guy driving it got off and started laughing. Only it didn't sound like a guy.

"What are you laughing at?" I demanded.

The guy took his helmet off. "He" was a girl! She had blue eyes and short blond hair, with bangs cut straight across her forehead. She was kind of pretty, I guess, and she looked as if she was about my age. Wouldn't you know it—the first person I met turned out to be a girl!

"You should watch where you step," she said, still laughing.

"Thanks for the advice."

"Who are you?" she asked. She took off her gloves and put them in her back pocket.

"My name's Billy."

"Did you just move here or something? I've never seen you around before."

I pointed back down the road. "Yeah, we just moved in. My dad inherited a farm from my great-grandfather," I told her.

She didn't say anything. She just nodded and started gathering dirt clods from alongside the road.

"Well, who are you?" I asked.

She flashed a goofy grin and put the clods down in a small pile at her feet. "Finally. I thought you'd never ask."

"So, what's your name?" I was starting to think she was kind of crazy.

She looked at me again with that funny smile. "Are you shy or something?"

"No, I'm *not* shy," I said. "It's just normal when you meet someone to tell them your name."

"Okay, okay, don't have a cow," she said. Then she started laughing.

"What are you laughing at now?"

"You didn't even get it. I said 'don't have a cow,' and that's all we have around here."

"I got it," I told her. "I just think cow jokes are, like, incredibly lame."

"That's because you don't get them," she said.

I decided to give this bizarre girl one last chance. "What is your stupid name?"

"For your information, my name is Fanny Rennet. And it's *not* stupid."

"Sorry, but you should just tell a person your name."

"Okay. My mom says I tease people too much." She picked up a dirt clod and heaved it at the guy on the sign.

"Why are you throwing dirt clods at that guy?"

"Because he's the evil-est guy in the world. He thinks he's, like, king of the town or something. And his nephew is a total jerk," she said, splattering mud all over the guy's face.

"Who is he?"

"Jonathan Curdle. He's the president of

IMP," she said. "Hey, do you have any special talents?"

Kids used to think I was pretty funny. I'm good at chemistry too. I used to make fizz bombs and stuff. I was about to answer when she cut me off.

"Because I do. I can make people barf whenever I want."

"No way," I challenged her.

"Yes way," she replied. "I could make you barf right here."

I didn't believe it. "All right," I said, crossing my arms in front of my chest, "go ahead."

"You'll be sorry."

"I'm not scared," I assured her.

She took a step back and started swallowing air in big gulps. Then she made a weird face and belched at me. A really long one.

It was the most horrible thing I had ever smelled. It smelled like rotten eggs and B.O. and asparagus and, worst of all, spoiled milk! I reeled back. My stomach churned. I got dizzy. I could feel slimy toast and orange juice rushing up my throat. Fanny danced away and started working up another burp. If she did it again, I would spew all over the road. I waved my arms at her.

"Don't do it again," I pleaded.

She laughed and stopped swallowing air. I

stood there for a moment, and the barf started to go down. When I felt okay, I leaned against a fencepost and looked at her. "That's pretty cool," I said.

"I know. I can do the grossest burps in town, maybe in the world," she boasted. Then she asked, "Are you going into town?"

"Yeah."

She got on her scooter. "C'mon, I'll give you a ride."

We buzzed down Main Street. There wasn't much traffic. Down one side street I glimpsed a big, modern glass-and-steel building. On the front of the building, it read IMP INTERNATIONAL HEADQUARTERS. The IMP building stood out because all the other buildings in town were really old-fashioned.

After a couple of blocks, Fanny pulled us up in front of the Moo 'n' Doo. I remembered the sign from when we arrived in town. There was a Donut Hut next door. As we got off the scooter, a fat cop came out with a dozen donuts.

"Hi, Officer Eclaire," Fanny said, waving.

"Hi there, Fanny. You be careful on that thing." He pointed at the scooter. His mouth was full of powdered sugar and chewed-up dough.

"I will," she promised. "This is Billy Fudder. His family just moved into Breakwind."

"Hi there, young fella. You stay out of trouble, you hear?"

"Okay. Nice to meet you, sir," I said.

He said something else, but his mouth was too full of donuts for me to understand.

Fanny pulled me toward the Moo 'n' Doo.

"My parents are kind of weird. But don't worry, they're nice anyway."

"Do your parents work here or something?" I asked.

"They own it," she said as she pushed the door open.

Inside were huge covered vats lined up along one wall. I didn't want to know what was in those vats. Across from them, along the other wall, were barber chairs.

"We used to have a farm," Fanny told me, "but IMP took it over. They won't stop until they own the town!"

I figured that was why she threw dirt clods at that ugly old guy's head.

"Fanny!" A man came out of a back room and walked over to us. He looked like a hippie. He was bald on top, but his hair was long on the sides and back. He had on a loose red shirt, purple pants, and sandals.

"Hi, Dad, this is Billy. He just moved to town with his family."

"Hi, Billy. Want a milkshake? We have twenty-three flavors."

Ugh. Fanny wasn't the only one in her family who could make me barf.

"Uh, no thanks," I said.

"All our shakes have a special ingredient," Fanny's dad continued. "Want to know what it is?"

"That's okay," I said. "I wouldn't want you to reveal your secret recipe or anything."

"Oh, it's not a secret," he said. "It's cheese."

"Cheese?"

"Dad—" Fanny began.

"That's right, Billy, cheese." This guy couldn't take a hint. "Have you ever tried a blue cheese shake?"

I tried to think about nice things—my posters, baseball...

"Or maybe you'd like to sample a Brie frappe," he went on. "Aged over a year!"

Just in the nick of time, I saw my dad driving down Main Street. "I'll be right back," I told them, and I ran outside.

Dad was stopped at a traffic light up the block. I ran up to the car. He had a big grin on his face. Fanny ran up behind me as my dad rolled down the window.

"What are you smiling about?" I asked.

"I have some great news for you."

"What, Dad, what?"

The light changed. Dad drove through the intersection and stopped in front of the Moo 'n' Doo. Fanny and I followed.

"I know you always wanted a brother," he said when we'd caught up. He was still grinning like an idiot.

Mom was pregnant!

"Now you're going to get the next best thing," he continued. "A brother-*in-law*. Your sister and Armand are engaged!"

CHAPTER
7

"Billy, Billy, don't look so shocked. Your old dad's just kidding!"

What a practical joker! I should've known.

"Hey, son, who's your friend?"

"This is Fanny Rennet," I told him. "Her parents own the Moo 'n' Doo."

"Pleased to meet you." Dad stuck his hand out the window and they shook hands.

"Hey, son," Dad said, "how would you like to earn a little extra money?"

"Doing what?"

"Cleaning out the basement at the old homestead. I'll pay you a dollar an hour. Your mom thought you might need a little spending money." He smiled at Fanny again.

"I don't know," I said. "Fanny and I were—" I didn't know what Fanny and I were going to do—or if we were going to do anything at all—but I sure didn't feel like cleaning out the basement.

"C'mon, Billy, I'll help you. It could be fun."

Fun? Cleaning out the basement? There must be less to do around Bledsoe than I'd thought. Woo-hoo, summer vacation!

"There you go, Billy, you've got a helper. I'll pay you a dollar an hour too, Fanny. What do you say?"

"Sounds good to me," she said before I could stop her.

"Okay, that's settled then. Climb on in and I'll drive you back."

"Why are you so into helping me clean out my basement?" I asked Fanny, looking around the old cellar. "This place is gross."

Fanny shrugged. "I don't know. You never know what you'll find. Besides, everyone knows that this was your great-grandpa's laboratory."

"Laboratory?"

"Yeah, he was some kind of mad scientist," she said, pushing a box over to the corner, where we were stacking them.

Dad hadn't said anything about him being a mad scientist—that was kind of cool.

"How do you know?" I asked her, opening a

box. There was an old gangster hat in it. I tried it on.

"He used to be the head of the milk-and-cheese research division at IMP, until the Curdles drove him insane or something. That's a cool hat," she commented. "Did you make sure there weren't any spiders in it?"

Spiders?! I took the hat off.

Then the lights went out!

It was pitch-black. I couldn't even see Fanny, who was standing right next to me. Then I felt something moving on my head.

"*Aaaaahhhhhhhhhhh*—spiders!" I screamed.

Fanny laughed. "It's just me, dummy."

"Give me a break," I told her.

"Got you!" she said.

"You did not. I just don't like people touching my head, that's all." I don't like spiders, either, but she didn't have to know that.

I walked over to the shuttered window and reached up. I could barely see it. I felt along the wall until I came to a little ledge.

"What are you doing?" Fanny asked from somewhere in the darkness.

"I'm just going to open the window." I put one foot on the ledge and made a jump for the latch and—I got it! Yes! Then I gave the latch a big shove and—

I fell off the ledge!

I hit the ground pretty hard. Fanny asked if I was okay. She sounded kind of worried.

Then the lights went back on.

Jennifer shouted from the top of the stairs, "Do I have your attention? It's lunchtime. Get cleaned up. We have company!"

My stupid sister had turned off the light!

I got up and dusted myself off. "I'll get you for this, metal-mouth," I yelled up the stairs.

"Look at that! There's a hole in the wall," Fanny gasped.

Right under the window, the brick I had stood on had fallen out. Fanny went over and started pulling out the other bricks. They came out pretty easily—and then we saw it: a metal pot, like a pressure cooker, and a dusty book!

"Billy, did you hear your sister?" Mom called. "Go and get cleaned up! We have visitors."

We didn't know anybody in town yet. Who could be visiting us?

Fanny was busy unscrewing the top of the pressure-cooker thing. I picked up the book. It looked like an old diary or something.

Fanny took the lid off the pot. Inside was a gray blob. "Look, Billy, it's a human brain!"

CHAPTER
8

"Wait a minute," I said after we'd both stopped screaming. I looked at the brain thing more closely. Then I poked it with my finger.

"Oh, that's so gross! Don't touch it!"

"It's not a brain," I told her. "It's cottage cheese."

Fanny looked at me wide-eyed. Then she looked at the cheese. "Really?"

"Yeah. I hate cottage cheese. That's the small-curd kind. I'd know it anywhere. Touch it."

Fanny hesitated, then poked the grayish mass. It kind of quivered. Then she did it again. It made a gooshy, slurping noise. When she pulled her finger out, there was no trace of the hole she had made.

"Billy, you kids come upstairs and get cleaned up now!" Mom yelled down the stairs again.

"What should we do with it?" Fanny asked.

"Let's just put the lid back on and come back down after lunch," I offered. "Maybe this book will tell us something."

Fanny pushed her finger into the cheese again. This time it quivered like Jell-O. There were more really gross slurpy noises when she pulled her finger out.

"That's cool," she said. "Try it."

I decided to just go for it, and shoved my index finger into the cheese. It felt really warm and gooey inside, like slimy oatmeal. There was something else too—a tickly feeling, like millions of maggots crawling up and down my finger. I pulled my finger out and the hole closed up.

I picked up the diary and read the first page. Scrawled across the top in capital letters, it read NOT FOR THE EYES OF ANY CURDLE! I showed it to Fanny and put it back in the wall just as Mom appeared at the bottom of the stairs.

"What is so interesting down here?" Mom demanded.

"Did you know that the basement was Great-Grandpa Theo's laboratory?" I asked her.

She didn't answer. "Didn't you hear me calling you guys?" she asked.

"Yeah, we heard you, Mom. But we found something really cool."

"Whatever you found can wait until you've had a nutritious lunch, Billy Fudder. You must be hungry too, Fanny."

Fanny nodded, but she didn't say anything.

"Mom, c'mere and look at what we found. It's really weird. It's like a brain made out of cottage cheese—"

"All right, Billy, that's enough. You march right upstairs and sit down for lunch. A brain made out of cottage cheese—what next?"

Fanny and I started for the stairs. Mom waited for us to go up first and followed.

"But, Mom, it's true. There's a diary too. I think it's Great-Grandpa Theo's." I looked at Fanny, but she was no help. "Come back down and look if you don't believe me. The diary says not to show it to any—"

As we emerged from the basement stairs into the back hall, I stopped dead in my tracks. Standing right in front of us was the old ugly guy from the sign. The guy Fanny had called the evilest man in the world—Jonathan Curdle!

He was even uglier in person. His head was all splotchy and his hands were all bony and veiny, with uncut yellow nails.

He looked at me—and lunged! I tried to back away, but Fanny was right behind me. I was trapped!

"Billy Fudder!" he cried as he grabbed at me. "I'm going to get you!"

CHAPTER
9

"What are you kids screaming about?" Dad asked, coming around the corner.

I ran over to him. "He said he was going to get me, Dad!"

Jonathan Curdle was standing in the hall, trying to look innocent.

"What in the world is the matter with you kids?" Mom asked.

"It's my fault," Jonathan Curdle said. "I'm afraid I must've frightened the lovable little tyke." He turned to me and smiled. His teeth were as jagged and yellow as his fingernails. "I only wanted to give you a hug, Billy. I loved your great-grandfather very much." He almost looked as if he was going to cry. "And you look so much like dear, departed Theo, I just couldn't help myself!"

Then I heard Jennifer's stupid voice from the

other room. "Where are you going, Jerry?"

Another guy came crowding into the hall. He was about my sister's age. He was a younger version of Jonathan Curdle.

"Oh, my dear nephew Jerry, come to my rescue. I am overcome at the sight of this little Billy Fudder." Jonathan Curdle collapsed in Jerry's arms.

I looked at Fanny. Jonathan Curdle didn't seem so evil to me now—just really ugly.

"And little Fanny Rennet, how are you, my dear?" he croaked.

"I'm fine," she said, staring him down.

Jonathan looked away. "I'm so tired."

"Why don't we all go back to the kitchen and calm down?" Dad suggested.

"First, I want Billy to apologize to Mr. Curdle," Mom said, looking at me.

Jonathan Curdle opened his red eyes.

"I'm waiting, Billy," Mom urged.

"I'm sorry, Mr. Curdle," I whispered.

The old man jumped out of his nephew's arms. "That's quite all right, young man. After all, we weren't properly introduced." He stuck out his gross hand. "Jonathan Curdle, IMP."

I zoned out as I took his cold, sweaty hand.

"Oh, yes, Theo and I were the best of friends," I heard Mr. Curdle saying as soon as I recovered from the shock. "We had our little differences, like everyone—but it was a loss to the whole town when he passed on."

Lunch was bologna sandwiches, which my mom kept apologizing for because she hadn't been expecting guests. Bologna was all right with me. Sandwiches are the one thing my mom can make.

Fanny and I sat down next to each other, across the table from Mr. Curdle and his nephew. Jennifer sat down next to Jerry Curdle. I could already tell she was in love with him. She kept flipping her hair and smiling at him in a weird way. I hoped we wouldn't find strands between the slices. He didn't even seem to notice her. He just kept stuffing sandwiches into his mouth until his uncle smacked him on the hand.

Fanny looked as if she were going to spew.

Then Mr. Curdle turned to Mom and said, "I understand you are in advertising, Ellen."

"Well, I was."

"It must've been hard to leave your career behind and move out to the middle of nowhere," Mr. Curdle commented.

"Well, it wasn't easy, but I go where my family goes. Besides, I thought it would be good for Billy and Jennifer to get out of the city—

country life and everything."

It's been real good so far, Mom. Thanks, I thought.

"How admirable! Family first, that's what I always say," Mr. Curdle announced. "However, I was wondering...If you ever find yourself with a little time to spare, perhaps you'd like to come over to IMP headquarters and have a look around our public relations department. It's small potatoes compared to what you're used to, but we could sure use some new ideas."

"I'd love to," she said. "I really won't be much help around here. I don't know anything about dairy farming."

About the last thing I wanted was for Mom to work for the Curdles! "Mom, you said you weren't going to work for a while."

Jonathan Curdle smiled at me. "We won't take your mom away, Billy. We'll just borrow her every once in a while. Would that be okay?"

"But you said you weren't going to work so much when we moved. You said you would be around more and learn how to cook and things like that."

"Oh, Billy, I'll still have plenty of time for you," she said, reaching over to pat me on the head.

"Maybe you could come work for us too, Billy," Mr. Curdle said suddenly. "You seem to have quite an imagination. What was it you were saying you found in the basement as you came up the stairs?"

"It was nothing." I told him. "Just a joke." No Curdles, the diary had said.

Mom laughed. "Tell us the joke now. A cheese that looks like a brain, or a brain that looks like a cheese, or something?

Mr. Curdle's red eyes were glowing.

"I was just kidding," I said. "There's just a bunch of old junk down there."

"What an imagination you have, Billy," Dad said. "You, too, Fanny?"

Fanny just smiled politely.

"Yes, a cheese that looks like a brain would be a rare find indeed, wouldn't it?" Mr. Curdle said. "Perhaps you could come to my office and tell me a story sometime. With an imagination like yours, it wouldn't take too much to entertain an old man like me, would it?"

"No, I guess not."

"Speaking of entertainment, what about this Dairy Dance we've heard so much about?" my dad asked.

"Oh, yes, the Dairy Dance," Mr. Curdle purred. "Just my little way of saying thanks to Bledsoe. You moved to our little town just in time."

"Who are you going to the dance with, Jerry?"

Jennifer asked, flipping her hair.

"Barble grrble duhbbldl," he answered through a mouthful of bologna sandwich mush.

"Dad, Fanny and I are finished. Can we go back down to the basement now?" I asked.

"Don't you want to hear more about the Dairy Dance?" Dad asked.

"I'd like to, but I really want to get that basement done."

Dad patted my head. Why was everybody patting my head all of a sudden?

"Okay, you and Fanny are excused."

Fanny and I got up and were heading toward the back hall when Mr. Curdle called out, "I'll see you kids around."

Not if I see you first, I thought. I looked at Fanny and knew she was thinking the same thing.

We raced down the basement stairs. Fanny beat me and ran across the cluttered floor toward the hole in the bricks. I ran after her—and my foot caught on a pipe.

"*Aaaaaaahhhhhh!*" I went down hard on the concrete floor. Next thing I knew, Fanny was screaming. "It's gone," she cried. "The cheese is gone!"

CHAPTER
10

"What do you mean, it's gone?" I groaned as I stood up and dusted myself off.

Fanny turned around and laughed. "Duuhhh. You are *so* gullible. What do you think, the cheese is just going to get up and walk away?"

"You should be on *America's Funniest Home Videos* or something—ha, ha, ha!" Then I looked at the cheese pot. But there was something different about it.

"Hey, Fanny, look at this," I said, kneeling. There was cheese all around the lip of the pot where the lid was screwed on.

"How did that get there?" she asked.

"I don't know," I said. I reached for the screws to take the lid off, but Fanny stopped me.

"Maybe you shouldn't take the lid off right now."

"Why not?" I asked. "Are you scared?"

"I'm not scared."

"Then let's open it up and see what's going on."

"But the diary said not to show it to any Curdles, and there's two of them right upstairs. What if they come down here?"

She had a point.

"Okay, what should we do with it?"

"There's an old abandoned barn out at the other edge of Breakwind where Chugachie State Park starts," she said. "Let's take it out there and then figure out what to do with it. No one will bother us."

"We have to get it out of the house first," I reminded her.

"With two of the hated Curdles up there, it won't be easy."

I snapped my fingers. "I got it. The window! You go outside and I'll hand it through the window to you!"

Fanny nodded and ran up the stairs. I found a wooden crate and put it under the window. Then I heard Fanny signal me and saw her black high-tops in the window. I reached into the hole in the wall for the cheese pot—I could barely lift it! I had to use all my strength to drag it out of the hole.

Fanny kept signaling for me to hurry up. I grabbed the pot with both hands, braced my feet, and lifted with all my strength. Somehow, I got it up on the box.

Fanny bent down and stuck her head in the window. "What are you waiting for?"

"It's really heavy all of a sudden, like it's gotten bigger or something," I said, trying to catch my breath.

Then I heard some voices, and Fanny frowned. "Keep low," she advised.

I heard my mom and dad and Jennifer saying good-bye to the Curdles. And then another pair of legs appeared in the window—Jerry Curdle!

"Hey, Fanny, you going to the dance with your daddy again?" he asked.

"Oh, go stuff it," she told him.

"Going with your daddy, going with your daddy!" he chanted.

I jumped up into the window and yelled, "Leave her alone, you stupid idiot!"

He jumped back, slipped on a big cow pie— *splat*—and fell on his back in a mud puddle.

"I'll get you for this, you little dork," he sputtered.

Then his uncle called him. "Jerry, dear nephew, come along! Come along now!"

Jerry looked at me and then got up. "You're

dead," he said, then stomped away. I heard a car start up.

Fanny poked her head in the window again. "Thanks," she said.

"What a jerk," I said.

"Yeah, he's a big jerk—he'll get you if he can."

"I'm not afraid of him."

"Ooh, big macho man," she teased. "You can't even lift that cheese up to the window!"

"Oh, yeah? Watch this!" I answered.

I bent down and grabbed the cheese pot with my feet apart. I braced myself and lifted. Slowly, I raised the cheese level with the window, grunting and gasping all the way. With one massive shove, I set it on the grass outside.

"That was pretty good, Arnold Schwarzenegger!" Fanny smiled at me. "Now let's get it out to the old barn."

Splat!

Man, was I going to be stepping in cow pies for the rest of my life?

"How did this thing get so heavy?" Fanny asked. We each had a handle. The cheese pot swung between us as we trudged to the old barn.

"I don't know. We didn't really lift it much in the basement. Maybe it was always this heavy and we just didn't notice."

"Could be—look, there it is." Across the pasture, backed right up against a tree-covered hill, was the old barn. The hill was the beginning of Chugachie State Park. Breakwind ended there.

As we got closer to the old barn I could see how run-down it was. The roof was half caved in, and the old red-and-white sliding door was off its track and tilting at a crazy angle.

"Let's rest for a minute," Fanny said, slowing down.

"We're almost there," I urged her on. I pulled on my side of the cheese pot and forced Fanny to trot behind me. After about two minutes, we stumbled into the shade of the old barn.

"Wow, this place is cool," I said. Rusted old-fashioned farm equipment hung from the walls and was scattered on the straw-covered ground.

"Yeah," Fanny gasped, collapsing onto an old wooden crate.

I pulled the diary out of my jeans jacket and leafed through it. There wasn't much there—some weird diagrams and formulas and a lot of blank pages. The only words were the ones at the beginning, warning about the Curdles.

"What's it say?" Fanny asked, brushing her blond hair away from her face.

"Not much." It was disappointing.

"Well, let's open the pot and look at the cheese again," Fanny suggested.

I nodded and we undid the top.

The cheese was bigger—there was no doubt about that. Before, it had just been sitting on the bottom of the pot. Now it was halfway to the top.

I reached in to touch it, then pulled my hand back in surprise. Had it moved?

"Did *you* see that?" I asked Fanny.

"What?"

"It moved. When I reached out to touch it, it kind of moved toward me."

Fanny stuck her hand in the pot and jammed her finger into the cheese. It quivered a little again, like Jell-O, but otherwise nothing.

"You're seeing things," she said. "It's just cheese. How could it move?"

"Well, how could it grow?" I argued. "There's something fishy about this cheese." The word "fishy" made me realize another thing. It didn't smell at all. I put my nose down close and took a big whiff—nothing!

"*Aahhhhhhhhhhhhhhhh!*" I screamed, jerking my head away from the pot.

"What? What's the matter!"

"It did move. I saw it—it moved!"

"Really?" she asked.

"Yeah, put your head down close and look."

She looked at me suspiciously and slowly moved her face down near the cheese. "I don't see anything—"

I put my hand on the back of her head and shoved her face into the cheese. When I let go, she came up with cottage cheese all over her face!

I was laughing so hard I didn't even notice her working up a huge burp. By the time I did, it was too late. She let go with a huge, honking stinker right in my face.

It worked instantly. I heaved all over the floor. She let go another one and I barfed again—big slimy chunks of bologna and white bread.

Then Fanny started laughing. My stomach really hurt, but I couldn't help laughing too. There was barf all over the floor and rotten cottage cheese all over Fanny's face. We laughed so hard we almost fell down.

Then I noticed something weird.

Cottage cheese curds had fallen off Fanny's face and landed in the vomit. When they hit the spew, they sat there for a minute, then started sizzling like an egg in a frying pan.

"It must be your weird enzyme," she said. Because I hadn't been able to drink the shakes at the Moo 'n' Doo, I'd told her about my stomach. I thought she was going to razz me about it, but she was really decent. "It's like acid to the cheese," she suggested.

I started to agree with her when we heard footsteps.

"Who's there?" I demanded.

Martha the cow poked her head around the corner of the barn door.

"It's only Martha," I said. "She's a weird cow, but she's harmless."

Fanny looked worried. "Everybody knows Martha," she whispered.

"What are you kids doing in here?"

Martha the cow was talking to us!

CHAPTER
11

Suddenly Armand came around the corner. "What are you kids screaming about?"

What a relief. It had been Armand talking— not Martha.

Armand had a big scowl on his face. He didn't look at all like the friendly weird guy in a tuxedo who I'd met the other night.

"We thought it was the cow talking," Fanny said, laughing. "We didn't see you."

Armand didn't laugh. He looked at Martha, who was just standing there chewing her cud. Then he pointed at our mess. His arm shot out of his sleeve like a missile and landed in my puke!

"Now look what you've done to my arm. And I just polished it. What are you doing out here, anyway?"

We were standing in front of the cheese pot so he couldn't see it. All of a sudden he had turned into a creep. He kept scowling at us and exchanging glances with Martha.

"We're not doing anything, we're just playing around," I said.

Armand shook his real finger at us as he retrieved his fake arm and wiped the puke off on the leg of his overalls. "You bratty kids, always screaming and making trouble. You shouldn't play out here. It's getting late—you go on home now."

That was too much! Breakwind was *my* farm now, even if I did hate it.

"We're not done with our, uh, game yet—we'll go home pretty soon," I told him.

I thought Armand was going to explode. His face got all red and he pushed his lank black hair out of his eyes. Then he smiled and said, "Oh, excuse me, the young master isn't done playing yet. Well, Martha and I will just leave you to your, uh, game." He clicked his fake arm back into place and turned to go.

Suddenly he spun around, his eyes bulging. "Just don't come crying to Armand when your little *game* blows up in your face."

Then he left. Martha trotted out after him without looking back.

"That guy should chill," Fanny said.

"No kidding."

Fanny looked at her Snoopy watch. "He was right, though. It's getting pretty late. I better get home."

Outside, it was just getting dark. We must have been there a long time. "You wanna meet up tomorrow?" I asked.

"I have to work at the Moo 'n' Doo until three," she told me. "Come by if you want."

"Okay," I said, "maybe I will."

We put the lid on the cheese pot and hid it under some boards. On the way back across the pasture, I stepped in three gooshy cow pies. A great way to end a great day.

The next day I wanted to go out and look at the cheese, but Dad kept me busy around the farm. Mom was at IMP talking to Mr. Curdle about a job. IMP was already taking over my family— just as Fanny had said it would. Armand wouldn't talk to me at all. When I said hi, he just scowled.

So when Dad asked me if I wanted to go into town with him to get some stuff, I jumped at the chance.

I went to the Moo 'n' Doo, but Fanny was out running some errands for her parents. I wandered around for a while and ended up in front of the Milk Museum. I was actually considering going in when I heard a voice behind me.

"Hey, dorkus."

It was Jerry Curdle!

"That's not my name," I told him.

"Well, what is your name? Peabrain? Pinhead? You ruined my good shirt, you know."

"You should watch where you step," I told him.

"You better shut up! Your great-grandfather was a nut, you know—a wacko! You're probably just as whacked out." He twirled his index finger by his ear and stuck his tongue out.

"Yeah? Well, at least he wasn't brain-dead like you," I shot back at him.

That shut him up. Then he grabbed me by the collar and lifted me off the ground!

CHAPTER 12

Suddenly, a police car squealed around the corner and Officer Eclaire stopped right beside us.

"Hey, you kids, what are you doing?" He rolled down the passenger-side window and shoved his fat face out. Beads of sweat rolled down his cheeks and neck.

"Uh, nothing, Officer Eclaire. We're just having a little fun," Jerry said, glaring at me.

Jerry relaxed his hold on me and I backed away from him.

"That's nice," Office Eclaire said. "Now I've got to be on my way. There's a big clearance sale at Donut Hut—fifty percent off everything. That's where I'm headed—you want a ride?"

I'm no snitch—but I wasn't going to wait around for Jerry to beat me into the ground, either. "I'll go with you," I offered. I started for the squad car.

Jerry grabbed me by the shoulder. "No thanks, Officer Eclaire," Jerry said, squeezing my shoulder hard. "It might spoil our lunch."

"You're a good boy, Jerry! You kids stay out of trouble, you hear?" Then he turned on his siren and sped off.

Jerry pounded his fist into the palm of his other hand and grinned at me.

"Now, Jerry, why don't we work this out like adults?" I reasoned with him. "Violence never solves anything, you know."

"I'm going to smash your head in, you little punk!" he said through his teeth.

"Well, it's been nice talking to you, Jerry—see you around!" I dodged to the right and then ran back around him to the left. I was home free—the street was wide open!

Then the creep stuck his leg out and I hit the asphalt. Not a good feeling.

Jerry stood over me with his hands on his hips. He looked positively evil. His eyes were on fire and his teeth looked like fangs!

"Get up, you little twerp!" he commanded.

Then I remembered a scene just like this in one of my favorite movies—*White Ninja Saves the World*. White Ninja, who is totally cool, is in a fight to the death with the evil Gekko. Gekko is about to win. He has White Ninja on the ground, when suddenly—

I jumped up and assumed a fighting position, letting out the fierce White Ninja war cry— *"Aaaaaahhhhhhhhhhhhhaaaaa!"*

"Man, you sure scream a lot," Jerry said. He picked me up by the collar again. "Let's go behind the Milk Museum, where no one can see us. We don't want anybody breaking this up."

CHAPTER 13

Jerry started dragging me, then suddenly stopped.

It was Martha and Armand, standing in the middle of the alley! Martha trotted forward and let out a big moo.

"What's going on here?" Armand demanded, shoving back his stringy black hair.

Jerry let go of me, and I scrambled over to Armand. "He was going to kill me," I explained.

Armand rolled his eyes. "You Curdles, you never can mind your own business, can you?"

"I wasn't doing anything! I was just joking, wasn't I, Billy—wasn't I?" He seemed really scared all of a sudden.

Martha trotted forward a few more steps until she was standing right in front of him. "Mooooooooo!"

"Call your cow off, Billy, call her off!" Jerry pleaded.

"You just get on out of here!" Armand shouted. "You just get on out of here and leave Billy alone, you punk!"

Martha took a half step forward. Jerry ran away as fast as he could.

"Hey, thanks, man," I said. "You too, Martha."

But what was Martha doing in town? Shouldn't she be on a leash or something? "Armand, what are you guys doing here?" I asked.

Armand looked at Martha and then back at me. "Oh, we were just passing by," he said.

"Why was Jerry so afraid of Martha?"

"You ask a lot of questions, guy," he said. "I guess you never heard of the great stampede of '89."

I shook my head.

"Jerry's folks got trampled in that dairy disaster," he explained. "Three whole herds took part in the ruckus, but the Curdles tried to pin the whole thing on Martha."

"Martha killed Jerry's parents?"

"Heck, no!" Armand exploded. "Why, if you believe that, you might as well—"

Martha interrupted him. "Moooo."

"Oh, never mind, just get out of here,"

Armand said. "And watch out for that Curdle—he's out to get you."

I nodded and turned to go.

Crossing Main Street, on the way to the Moo 'n' Doo, I heard an engine racing down the street. I turned just in time to see a car hurtling toward me!

CHAPTER
14

The station wagon squealed to a halt inches in front of me. Dad sat grinning behind the steering wheel. What a joker!

I started to get into the car when I heard the telltale buzzing of Fanny's scooter. She skidded to a halt next to the station wagon and smiled.

"Hi, Fanny," I said.

"What are you doing?" she asked, shaking hands with Dad.

"We're going out to paint the old homestead," Dad informed her. "Want to join us?"

"I can't. I have to help my folks clean out the Moo 'n' Doo. Health inspector's coming tomorrow. Just one hair in the strawberry shake vat, and they'll close us down like last year."

"What are you doing tomorrow?" I asked her as Dad revved the engine.

"No plans. How about you? Are you going to be painting all day?"

"We'll see how much we get done," Dad said. "I suppose I could let him off for good behavior tomorrow, the little buckaroo!"

Little buckaroo? Hello?

"Okay, I'll call you tomorrow. We can go fishing near the old barn," she said, giving me a big obvious wink.

The old barn.

Dad hit the gas and we squealed away from Fanny and out into the wide open country.

Mom still wasn't back from IMP when we got home. But she'd left a message on the answering machine saying that she was already involved in a big project there and she wouldn't be back until late.

Jennifer was out with Jerry—okay by me.

It was kind of nice just painting the house for the rest of the afternoon. Armand helped, but still acted weird. Whenever I tried to ask him more about what had happened earlier, he only said there was work to do.

So we just painted. The big oak tree in the front yard waved a little in a breeze that cooled us down when the sun got too strong.

I was painting the trim on the big front-room

window when Dad pointed at the big oak tree.

"You know, that tree looks perfect for a treehouse, doesn't it?" he asked.

I wiped the sweat off my forehead with the back of my hand, which was speckled with light blue paint, and looked at the tree. Dad was right—there were branches about halfway up that forked just right. I could probably build a better one than Tommy and I had!

"As soon as we get the house squared away, maybe we could draw up some plans," Dad suggested.

"Yeah, Dad, that would be great."

"Are you liking Bledsoe any better these days?"

It was such a nice afternoon, I had almost forgotten about that slimeball Jerry. I thought about how cool Fanny was—I would have to ask her if she liked White Ninja movies. And the whole cottage cheese thing was a real mystery. It looked as if it might be an interesting summer after all.

"Yeah, Dad, I guess I am," I told him.

"Glad to hear it, son. How about a nice cold glass of lemonade?"

I nodded and he said, "Good. Get me one while you're at it!"

*   *   *

The next day I talked to Fanny in the morning and she came over. Dad had to talk business with the people at his company, Aquariumania, so Fanny and I had some time to check out the old barn.

"Do you like White Ninja movies?" I asked her as we crossed the pasture.

"I've only seen one, but I thought it was pretty good."

"Which one?" I asked eagerly. I felt like jumping up and down, but I forced myself to be cool.

"*The White Ninja Returns*, or something like that."

I couldn't believe it. This was my day! "*The White Ninja Returns*? Really? That's one of the best movies ever made. That's the one where Gekko brings the White Ninja back from the dead and tries to turn him into a slave of evil!"

"Yeah, it was pretty cool. I liked the girl—"

"Doreen?"

"Yeah, Doreen, that's it."

"Oh, man, I love that movie!" I told her. I did a couple of karate kicks and yells and—*splat!* My foot landed right in a big steamy cow pie.

"Smooth move, ninja!" Fanny howled.

I shook my head and wiped the cow doo on the grass.

"Anyway I have all the White Ninja movies at

home on video if you want to watch them some-time," I offered.

We walked the rest of the way to the old barn in silence. I had to concentrate on the ground. I didn't feel like stepping on any more land mines.

We went into the barn. There was definitely something wrong with this cheese! We had put the lid back on, but now it was off! It was lying beside the cheese pot—and the cheese had grown some more! Now it was overflowing the rim of the pot.

"Who do you think took the lid off?" Fanny asked.

"Armand, I guess."

Then a bubble formed, rising out of the cheese and bursting with a burping sound.

"That's weird," Fanny said, reaching toward the cheese. "Sounds like me."

I grabbed her hand and held her back. "Don't touch it anymore!"

"Man, what a chicken," she said, plunging her hand into the curdy mess. "It feels kind of different—less gooshy."

"*Aaahhhhhh!*" she suddenly screamed. "It's got me, it won't let go, help!"

I grabbed her arm and pulled and pulled. Then Fanny started laughing. "Oh, help me, White Ninja, help me, White Ninja!"

"Really hilarious!" I yelled at her.

"You were so scared."

"I was not. I knew you were kidding." I crossed my arms. *Stay cool.*

"You did not."

"I did too. Just get your hand out of the cheese!" I grabbed her by the wrist and yanked her hand out.

We both froze!

The cheese stretched. A tentacle of cheese wrapped around her arm and belched as she pulled her hand away. Fanny moved her hand and the cheese stuck to her, quivering a little but holding fast.

Then it moved. It definitely moved. It wrapped farther up Fanny's arm and then uncoiled, retracting back into the pot—*splooc-chh!*

"Fanny, are you all right?"

"Yeah," she said. "It didn't hurt me. It felt kind of cool. Try it."

I held my palm over the cheese for a few seconds. "Nothing," I said, laughing nervously.

Fanny shrugged and smiled. "I guess you have to touch it."

"Maybe."

Then the cheese grabbed me! It shot up and splooched onto my hand and wriggled around until it had covered my fingers. I almost screamed, but it didn't seem as if it wanted to hurt me. Fanny was right—it felt kind of nice.

It slithered around my hand, as if it was exploring, then retracted back into the pot.

"That's the coolest cheese I ever saw!" Fanny said.

It was pretty cool. But it was still growing. I was more suspicious of this cheese than Fanny was.

"Maybe we ought to tell somebody about this or something," I suggested.

Fanny shook her head. "No way. You remember what happened to E.T. Anyway, then the Curdles would find out about it. And the diary said, specifically, no Curdles!"

Just then we heard a flapping noise and looked up. A bird—a robin, I think—had flown into the barn. It flapped around and then landed on one of the rotted-out rafters.

"Maybe we can train the cheese to do tricks," Fanny said.

I looked at Fanny and we laughed. Then we heard the sploochy noise and the cheese shot out another tentacle. We jumped back and watched as it shot up toward the roof, grabbing the bird off the rafter! The chesse snapped back into the pot. Then there was another bubble, the cheese burped, and the bird disappeared.

So much for cool cheese!

Out of nowhere a voice said, "You've made an exciting discovery, children—but also a dangerous one."

"Did you hear that?" Fanny whispered.

I nodded and looked around the barn. There was no one else there. Then Martha trotted in and looked at us with her big brown eyes.

"It must've been Armand," I cried. "He's spying on us!"

CHAPTER
15

I ran past Martha and out the door. There was no one out there. Everything was quiet. The cows were in the pasture.

I walked back into the barn to tell Fanny. Something was wrong. She was staring weirdly at Martha.

"What's wrong?" I asked.

She didn't answer, just slowly raised her hand and pointed at Martha.

The old cow swung her large head around and regarded me silently. "Yes, Billy, it is I, Martha," she said in a low voice. I was hearing it but I wasn't believing it. Martha was a cow—and cows can't talk!

"Let's get out of here, Billy!" Fanny cried.

"Do not be frightened, children. I will not harm you in any way." Martha's thin cow lips were moving!

"We're not children," Fanny snapped. "Billy's twelve and I'm almost thirteen!"

"You are children to me," Martha said. "I am very old."

"You're also a murderer!" Fanny shouted.

The great stampede of '89! Jerry Curdle's parents!

"I am not a murderer," Martha explained calmly. "That stampede was supposed to have been a peaceful demonstration of our strength."

"Whose strength?" I demanded.

"The cattle of Bledsoe," Martha said matter-of-factly. "IMP had been running secret experiments on us for years. It had to stop! Unfortunately, there are always a few hotheads in any herd. I tried to keep them under control. It is one of the great regrets of my life that I was unable to do so."

"But how can you talk?" I asked.

"I am one of your great-grandfather's greatest experiments, Billy. I am not even sure if *he* knew how he did it—I can't tell you. One moment I was chewing my cud in the pasture with the other cows. The next moment, I was...different!" Martha's voice was sad.

"You must not reveal my secret to anyone," she warned. "All these years, only your great-grandfather and Armand have known the truth."

Armand and Martha. Things were starting to make sense.

"But why are you telling us?" Fanny demanded. "Aren't you afraid that a couple of *children* won't be able to keep your secret?"

Martha trotted forward a little. "I am telling you now because you have found the cheese."

"The cottage cheese?" I asked.

"Yes. It was another one of Theo's experiments—and one which must be destroyed!"

"But why?" Fanny asked. "I think it's kind of cute!" She walked back over to the cheese pot and put her hand over it. The cheese reached out a tentacle and seemed to stroke her arm gently.

"It is harmless for the time being, I think," Martha said. "But I must study the diary carefully. I do not not wish to destroy any form of life— I am something of a freak myself. I don't even know if it can be destroyed. I must see the diary."

I dug the old book out of its hiding place and put it down in front of Martha.

"But why can't the Curdles know about it?" I asked.

Martha turned and looked at me with her deep brown eyes. "No one must know about it— especially not the Curdles! The cheese was developed by Theo in their laboratories. He thought he was working for the good of mankind. But Jonathan Curdle would have turned his creations to evil, so he quit and continued his experiments at home, in the basement. There is no telling what despicable use Jonathan Curdle would put the cheese to if he learned of its existence!"

"But what do we do now?" Fanny asked.

"First, we put the cheese back into its container," said Martha. "Then I will study the diary—perhaps together we can control it."

Fanny and I nodded. Then I looked at the cheese pot and gasped. The cheese had outgrown the pot and was oozing over the sides!

"Hurry, children!"

We scooped up big handfuls of cheese and dumped them back into the pot. Bubbles formed and burst on the surface. There was something else too—the cheese was starting to stink. I kept gagging, and thought I was going to heave.

Finally, we got all the cheese back into the pot and stuffed it down. Fanny grabbed the lid and tried to put it on—but the cheese fought back!

I pushed too, with all my strength! The lid started to go down, then leaped up again. We kept pushing, but it was no use.

Then, with a crazed look in her eye, Martha charged us!

CHAPTER
16

"Stand back, children!" Martha bellowed.

She lifted her front hooves and pounded them down on the lid, squashing down the cheese and almost squashing us!

"Now secure the screws!"

We did as we were told. We stuck the screws in place and spun them around as fast as we could. Finally, the cheese was locked in.

"All right, children, go home now," Martha said. "I need time to study the diary—and think."

We walked back across the pasture toward my house. The crickets chirped. A distant cow mooed. We didn't say anything as we walked. I guess we were both trying to calm down.

Suddenly a dark form ran past us, heading toward the barn.

"Wait a minute," Fanny said. "That's Jerry Curdle."

I was about to run the other way when Fanny shouted, "Stop!"

Jerry stopped running and walked toward us.

"Hi, Billy. Hi, Fanny," he said, panting.

"What are you doing here, Jerry?" Fanny asked. "And where are you running to?"

"Me and Jennifer are going to the movies. I was just getting in a quick run." He turned to me and said, "Hey, sorry about the other day. You're a pretty tough kid. I like you."

Fanny and I glanced at each other, and then back at Jerry.

"Did I hear you saying you guys were fooling around at the old barn?" he asked casually.

I stepped forward. "Yeah, we're going to turn it into a clubhouse—the No Jerrys Allowed Club!" I heard Fanny laugh behind me.

I thought Jerry was going to take a swing at me when I made the "No Jerrys" crack. But he just stood there smiling. I didn't trust him for one minute.

"That's pretty funny, kid. The old barn's dangerous, though. Maybe I could come out there with you sometime."

"Sure, Jerry, you can help," Fanny said. "As soon as my cousin Marcy writes me a letter that says her pig is flying!"

Jerry's face scrunched up for a second. I

thought for sure he was going to hit one of us. But he just laughed again.

"Why don't you guys tell me what's really going on out there at the old barn? Jennifer says that's where you're spending all your time."

Stupid Jennifer! What a big mouth!

"Nothing. We're just going to turn it into a clubhouse, like I said," I told him.

Jerry chuckled and pulled a leaf off a low-hanging branch. He crumpled it in his hand, then hurled it to the ground. "Just a couple of kids playing around, huh?"

"Yeah," I assured him.

"Playing around—with cheese?"

I was about to deny everything when the screen door crashed open. "Billy!" Jennifer shrieked from the porch. "I want to talk to you. You stay right there!"

Oh, great. What now?

She tripped across the front yard, wearing a tight new dress and high heels. She also had a lot of makeup on—but it only made her zits stand out.

"Billy," she screamed. "You stop pestering Jerry!"

Hello?

"He told me how you sicced that horrible old cow on him the other day."

"It's okay, it was no big deal," Jerry said, as if he was a nice guy instead of a cretin.

Jennifer smiled at Jerry. "Let's go. Our movie starts pretty soon. And don't forget what I said, you little runt!" she called over her shoulder as they walked to Jerry's car.

"You want to watch a White Ninja movie?" I asked Fanny.

"Sure," she said. "I want my moves to be super-smooth the next time we bump into that dude."

The next day, Fanny and I headed out to the barn. It was a great day. The sun was warm and the sky looked like a postcard.

Suddenly, Fanny cried, "Billy, look!"

The old barn was shaking. The whole thing rumbled and rocked back and forth, and this horrible smell floated toward us—rotten cheese!

"What's going on?" I started running toward the old barn. We were almost there when a red plank flew at us.

"Get down," Fanny cried, and we ducked for cover.

Suddenly, the old barn exploded!

When we looked up again, we saw a huge white form growing out of the rubble. It made ear-shattering burping and sucking noises as it rose up toward the sky. Then it started toward me and Fanny!

As it advanced, the cheese grew so enormous that it blotted out the sun.

"Mommmmmmmmmmm!"

CHAPTER 17

"Billy, honey, wake up!"

I opened my eyes. Mom was kneeling next to my bed. Her hand rested on my forehead.

"Oh, Mom!" I cried, hugging her.

"My goodness, what happened?" she asked, hugging me back.

I let go of her and shook my head. "I had a bad dream, that's all."

"Well, it must've been pretty awful. I just came up here to kiss you good-bye before I went to work, and you started screaming."

"Mom, please don't go back to IMP," I said.

She smiled at me and stood up. "I know I said we would spend more time together after we moved, but I didn't know this job would come up. Anyway, I'm only going to work on this one campaign and that's it."

"What campaign?" I asked, rubbing the sleep out of my eyes.

"The new town slogan," she said proudly. "What do you think of this?" She took a few steps back and raised her arms. "'Think Cheese—Think Bledsoe!' Catchy, huh?"

"It's okay," I mumbled.

She let her arms fall to her sides. "Well, we're still working on it," she admitted.

"Can't you just stay home, Mom? I don't want you going back to IMP."

"Billy, you're too old for this. You know how much I enjoy my work. Besides, we have to have the slogan ready for the Dairy Dance, so it's only a couple of days more."

She looked around my room. With everything going on, I still hadn't put my posters up.

"I'll tell you what. When I'm all done at IMP, I'll help you decorate your room. What do you say? We'll paint it and everything. Any color you like."

"Okay."

"Good, that's settled." She kissed me on the cheek. "Have a cheese day, sweetheart."

"What did you say, Mom?"

"I said 'Have a nice day, sweetheart.' What did you think I said?"

*   *   *

After breakfast I went into town to talk to Fanny. I had a really important question to ask her.

"It was all a dream, wasn't it?"

"Sure seems like it," she said.

We sat at the counter in the Moo 'n' Doo. She drank a Parmesan shake. I pinched my nostrils so I wouldn't have to smell it and had a Coke.

"I mean, there's no such thing as a talking cow, right?" I asked.

"I've never heard of one...before Martha," she said, slurping her shake. It was pretty early, so we were the only ones at the counter. Fanny's dad was in the back cutting Nurse Pontiac's hair. She was IMP's company nurse, and barely fit in the barber chair.

"Because I've been thinking," I said, breaking the silence. "There was this part in the first White Ninja movie where the White Ninja was hypnotized. He thought he was back in, like, old Japan, but he was really in Las Vegas, under the power of Gekko."

"You think somebody hypnotized us?" she asked.

"Maybe it was a hallucination or something," I told her. "I'm going back out there to find out."

Fanny brought her glass down on the marble

counter with a loud crash. "All right, I'm going with you!"

We rode her scooter back out to my house and marched across the pasture. I didn't step in any cow stuff on the way. That made me feel better. The barn was just a stupid old abandoned barn—no talking cows in sight.

"I think I was right," I began as we stepped through the old sliding door. "It must've been some kind of weird dream, like last night."

"*Aaaaaaahhhhhhhhhh!*" Fanny screamed.

There was Jerry Curdle standing in the middle of the barn. A ray of sunlight streamed through a hole in the roof, glinting off the pocketknife in his hand.

CHAPTER
18

"Jerry, we're sorry about the cracks yesterday," I said, looking at the knife. "We were just kidding around, you know?"

"Forget about it." He took a step forward.

"Don't stab us, Jerky—I mean, Jerry!" Fanny shrieked.

"I'm not going to stab you, you little runt. I didn't bring the knife for you. I brought it for this!" He reached down and and hefted the cheese pot onto an old barrel. The lid was off, and it looked as if the cheese had shrunk a little. It was quivering—almost as if it was afraid. And boy, did it stink!

"Jerry, that cheese could be dangerous," I informed him.

"I know all about it. My uncle's been looking for this thing for years. He wasn't even sure if it really existed. Your great-grandfather stole all the molecular models and formulas when he quit IMP. But now I've found it! Culture 286!"

"Culture 286?" Fanny and I asked at the same time.

"That was its code name. I overheard you little dorks talking yesterday and I remembered what you said that first day my uncle brought me out here with him. When I show this to him, he's probably going to make me a vice president at IMP. I'll be a senior executive before I'm a senior in high school!"

Jerry held his knife over the cheese. The cheese trembled, expanding and contracting in its pot, as the ambitious teenager moved toward it.

"I'd take it all off your hands, but it's a little heavy. So if you don't mind, I'll just take a sample for now." Jerry laughed, searching the cheese for a likely spot to cut.

He raised the blade, laughing even louder.

"Jerry, don't cut the cheese!" I screamed. But it was too late!

The knife went in. He hacked a piece out and held it up for us to see.

"This is going to make me famous," he announced, squishing the cheese between his fingers.

Then the cheese burped and began rising out of the pot. It expanded until it topped Jerry by a good two feet.

"Aaaaaaaahhhhhhhhhhhhhhhhh!"

"What are you punks screaming about now?" Jerry demanded, whirling around to see what we were pointing at.

CHAPTER
19

"Aaahhhhhhh!" Now Jerry was screaming, too.

The cheese trembled in the air above Jerry. He dropped the knife and the piece of cheese. The cheese collapsed on him with a satisfied belch that stank so bad we had to hold our noses.

Then the cheese started to move again. It rose up and started to take on human form! Jerry's face appeared in its midsection for a second. His mouth moved in silent cries for help. Then he vanished!

The cheese continued to re-form itself. Culture 286 stood there in front of us, looking like the misshapen body of Jerry Curdle!

Fanny and I took a few steps back. I felt her hand reaching for mine and I grabbed it.

The cheese advanced on us. Suddenly, it raised its cheesy arms and attacked!

CHAPTER 20

"Get behind me, children, and stop screaming!"

It was Martha. She trotted forward and stood between us and the cheese.

The cheese took a few small steps toward Martha. Clods of curds cascaded down, splatting on the wooden floor.

Then it stopped.

Martha stared at the cheese monster. Her eyes bored into what would have been its face—if it had a face, instead of a mass of squishy cottage cheese!

Then the monster belched, raised its arms over its head and ran out of the barn, leaving behind a trail of rotten cheese.

So much for that dream theory of mine, I figured.

"Is Jerry dead?" Fanny asked Martha frantically.

The old cow's eyes were gentle again, and a little sad.

"No, Fanny, I don't think Jerry is dead. He has been absorbed. It is only a matter of time, though, until Culture 286 starts digesting him—" The cow didn't finish.

"What happened to it?" I asked. "Why did it go crazy?"

"When the cheese absorbed Jerry, it absorbed his evil with him. There is no telling what it will do now!"

"We have to do something," I said. "We have to go find it!"

"No!" Martha cried. "You can't stop it now—it is out of your hands."

"Martha, why did the cheese stink so bad all of a sudden?" I asked. "I thought I was going to heave for a minute there."

"It is rotting. It must replenish itself. Non-fat cottage cheese cannot go long without feeding! It must find fresh cheese—or it will die."

"No problem, then," Fanny said. "All we have to do is wait for it to die."

"Yes, it will die," Martha said. "Eventually."

Fanny gulped. "Eventually?"

"We have to do something," I cried. "We can't just let Jerry be digested!"

"*I* could," Fanny said.

"Please," Martha said. "I need more time.

Give me another day. There must be a way—and it must be in that diary!"

Fanny and I nodded and left the barn. We headed for home, but not before crossing the trail of squishy cheese leading into the state park.

"Where is it?" I was emptying boxes and throwing clothes all over my bedroom floor.

"What are you looking for?" Fanny asked, bouncing up and down on my bed. She looked around at the bare walls. "You're sure not much of a decorator."

"Well, I haven't had all the time in the world, you know," I snapped.

"Don't get mad at me," she said.

"I'm not mad at you, I just—there it is!" I reached into the back of the closet and pulled out a big, colorful cardboard box.

"The White Ninja Action Set? That stuff's for babies!"

"It is *not* for babies," I said. "Anyway, I haven't played with it in years."

"Oh, yeah, try last month," she shot back.

I pulled the nunchaku out of the box and whirled it in the air. I slammed it down on the bed next to Fanny.

"Hey, watch it!" she cried, jumping up. "That

thing is dangerous."

"Chill. I'm an expert."

"But why are you getting it out now?" Fanny said, hefting the nunchaku in one hand.

"I'm going after that cheese," I told her.

"But Martha said—"

"Martha is a cow," I told her, wrapping the White Ninja Assault Turban around my head. "And I can't sit around while she tries to solve my problems."

"What are you going to tell your parents?"

"That I'm going for a little camping trip in Chugachie State Park."

"I'm going with you," Fanny declared, flicking a throwing star so that it buried itself an inch deep in my dresser.

"Hey, watch it," I cried. "My mom will freak."

"Sorry about that," she said.

I'd never admit it, but that was a pretty good throw!

When we had everything together, we went downstairs to stock up on supplies.

Dad came into the kitchen and said, "You kids are pretty hungry, huh?"

"We're going camping out in Chugachie for the night," I told him.

"Camping, huh? That's great. It's the only

way to really appreciate Bledsoe—get out and see it! But you be careful, huh?"

"We will," Fanny and I said together. We loaded our stuff into two packs and headed out.

There was no sign of Martha as we trudged acoss the pasture, past the old barn, and into the park.

"What are we going to do when we find it?" Fanny asked as we entered the forest.

I stopped and pushed my Assault Turban back on my head. It kept falling down over my eyes. And since it was already starting to get dark, I almost ran smack into a tree because of the stupid thing.

"I don't know—conquer it, I guess," I replied. Shadows stretched between the trees. The woods were alive with buzzing and crackling sounds.

"I'm hungry," Fanny said.

"You're hungry already? We just got here."

"So what? Let's eat!"

"We can't eat now." I told her. "We have to find the cheese monster." Someone had to lay down the law.

"Okay," she said. "But as soon as we find the stupid thing and conquer it or whatever, then we get to eat, all right?"

"Okay." I nodded. My Assault Turban fell

back down over my eyes.

"Aaahhhhhhhh!" Fanny screamed. "What's that?"

I whirled around, trying to push my Assault Turban back on top of my head. The pin came out of the turban and it started to unwind. Suddenly, something caught at my foot!

CHAPTER 21

"Aaaaaahhhhhhhhhhhh!" I cried as I fell to the forest floor.

Fanny was silent. Had the evil cheese claimed its latest victim?

"Fanny?" I whispered.

Then she started laughing. I pulled the folds of the turban away from one eye. A bright light practically blinded me. It was Fanny shining her flashlight in my face.

"Just testing your reflexes, White Ninja," she said.

"Don't do me any favors," I said, wrapping the Assault Turban back around my head. After I had pinned it in place, I shot my balled fist toward Fanny's face.

"Made you flinch!" I cried, laughing.

"Did not!"

Suddenly, I smelled something that almost

made me hurl chunks all over the forest! "You smell that?" I asked, motioning for her to be quiet.

She sniffed the air and nodded. It was too weak to be the actual monster, but it had definitely been there.

Then I found it—a cheesy trail. It was already all moldy and disgusting, but it was a good lead.

"I think it went that way," she said, pointing ahead, farther into the forest. I got my flashlight out and switched it on.

We walked for about two hours. The night got darker and darker. Our flashlights were pretty powerful, but we could only see a little ways ahead of us because of the dense trees. The trail got fresher as we kept going—we knew we were on the right track.

A forest can be pretty scary at night. There's all kinds of sounds. You don't know where they are coming from. The shadows are all deep and black and anything could be hiding in them.

Suddenly, I took a step, and *splat!*

"Oh, no, not again." I shined my flashlight down, but it wasn't a cow pie. It was a big mound of gunky cheese. "We must be close," I whispered.

Fanny shined her flashlight into the darkness. A pile of something green and shiny lay directly ahead of us. "What's that?" she asked.

We walked over to it. It looked like a nest—made of iceberg lettuce. There was rotten cottage cheese everywhere.

"This must be where it sleeps," I said. "But why is its bed made out of lettuce?"

"Cottage cheese and iceberg lettuce go together. Haven't you ever seen those diet plates that ladies order in restaurants?"

"Cottage cheese on a bed of lettuce—my grandma used to get that all the time."

"Exactly," she said.

Suddenly, Fanny spun around, peering into the darkness of the woods. "What was that?" she whispered.

"Turn your flashlight off so it can't see us." I flicked my light off at the same time.

We stood there in the dark, listening. A twig broke. Dry leaves crunched not too far away. My heart was pounding. I slid my nunchaku out of my pack. In the dim moonlight I could barely see Fanny getting the throwing stars ready.

As my eyes adjusted, I made out a shadowy figure on the other side of the lettuce nest. I nudged Fanny in the ribs.

"Ready," she said.

We took a couple of steps foward—and the monster attacked!

CHAPTER 22

I ran at the horrible cheese, the stink of its decaying body filling my nostrils. I whirled the nunchaku. Fanny hurled the throwing stars.

"*Oowwwwww!*" the cheese monster cried as the nunchaku connected with its slimy body.

"The cheese said 'ow'?" I asked no one in particular.

"Stop it, you kids," the cheese monster said. "I'm here to help!" I shined my flashlight on the dark figure.

Armand!

Ker-thunk! A throwing star planted itself in Armand's arm.

"Fanny, wait, it's Armand!"

Fanny came forward into the light. "Sorry about that, Armand."

"It's all right," Armand said, pulling the star out of his arm.

"Good thing it was your fake arm," she said.

"Sure is," he said, patting it.

"What are you doing out here?" I asked him.

"I came to help you. I tried to scare you away from messing with the cheese by being mean, but it didn't work."

So *that's* why he'd been acting so weird.

Armand picked up a stick and doodled on the damp forest floor. "Then I thought, it's their problem. Let those kids figure it out—sink or swim, that's how I always got along!"

He paused and looked around. "But I couldn't. I told Theo that Culture 286 was dangerous and should be destroyed!" He raised the stick over his head and snapped it in half. "But he wouldn't listen. Martha thinks she can figure something out from the diary. But most of it is in code, in case any Curdles got ahold of it! So now here I am to finish what I started."

"What you started?" I asked.

"Well, what I started with Theo. I was his assistant!"

Then I heard this kind of smooshy sound behind me and smelled something disgusting.

I spun around and grabbed Fanny.

It was towering over us! Chunky Cheese!

CHAPTER 23

"*Aaaaaaaaaahhhhhhhhhhhhhh!*" the cheese roared at us. Slobbering slimy chunks of rotten cheese dripped out of a hole in its head on long strings of mucus.

I thought we were goners. We'd already unloaded all of our ninja weapons on Armand.

The monster tottered forward and took a swipe at us. I pulled Fanny back just in time.

And then Armand jumped between us and the cheese.

"Take me!" he screamed, charging at the cheese.

"Armand!" Fanny yelled, but it was too late. There was a squishy sound, and the cheese monster slumped a little as it sucked Armand in.

As he started to disappear, he cried, "Save

yourselves, kids. Run! Run away and don't look back!"

"No, Armand, we won't leave you!" I cried. Armand was almost gone when I let go of Fanny and reached for his arm, still sticking out of the now shapeless mound of cheese. I pulled on Armand's arm, trying not to barf from the monster's putrid smell.

"Pull harder!" Fanny cried.

Suddenly I was flying backward through the air—Armand's arm had come off!

At least we'd have something to remember him by if we couldn't get the rest of him out.

The cheese burped, then started to pull itself back together.

I jumped to my feet. "Let's get out of here!"

"We have to tell somebody," I told Fanny as we stood at the front gate of IMP's international headquarters the next day. "It's swallowed two people now. We can't handle this on our own."

"What are you going to say—that there's a giant cottage cheese on the loose?"

It was morning by the time we made it out of the woods. We were covered with scratches and bruises. I had lost my Assault Turban somewhere in the woods. And we had been arguing all the way into town.

"Besides, she works for the Curdles now," Fanny sneered.

"She's still my mom," I said. "I'll make her believe me!"

A pickup truck rumbled down the street, headed for Main. And standing in the bed was Culture 286, its arm raised to smash down on the roof of the cab!

CHAPTER
24

"Aaaaaahhhhhhhhhhhh!" A voice screamed with us, right behind us.

I spun around. It was Officer Eclaire.

"Hey, that's kind of fun. No wonder you kids are screaming all the time. What are we screaming about?" the police officer asked, scratching his bald head with the visor of his cap.

"There, in the back of that truck," I said, pointing. "It's a monster. Stop it!"

Officer Eclaire laughed and put his cap back on. "It *is* a monster—a monster of a cottage cheese sculpture! It's the biggest one ever. You can get a better look at it tonight at the Dairy Dance."

The Dairy Dance! Tonight!

"Well, I guess I'll see you kids tonight!" Officer Eclaire said, walking away.

I was relieved that it wasn't the monster. Then I thought of something that scared me even more.

"Hey, Fanny, remember what Martha said about the cheese having to replenish itself?"

"Yeah."

"Well, where's the most cottage cheese in the world going to be tonight?"

"The Dairy Dance," she gasped.

I nodded. The cheese would not be able to resist the sculpture. The whole town would be gathered in one place. I had to tell somebody!

"I'm going to tell my Mom. She'll help us," I said.

"Good luck," Fanny said. "I'd come along, but after the Curdles bought out our family farm, I vowed never to set foot in that building."

"Billy, what happened to you?" Mom asked when she spotted me.

I ran to her down a long line of desks. "Mom, something really bad has happened!"

"Wait one minute," she said excitedly. "Just listen to this new slogan we came up with today."

"But, Mom—"

"Ready? 'Bledsoe—It's the Cheesiest!' "

"That's great, Mom. Now listen, please!"

"How did you get all scratched up, Billy?" she

asked, grabbing me by the chin and turning my face toward her. "And on the night of the Dairy Dance, too. You better go home and start getting cleaned up. We have to be there a little early to help set up—I'm going to be presenting the new town slogan, you know."

"But, Mom, we have to stop the Dairy Dance!"

"Stop the Dairy Dance? Why?"

"Look, I know this is going to be hard to believe, but there's this monster—it's made out of cottage cheese. Its code name is Culture 286. Great-Grandpa Theo invented it, and—"

"Not that cheese brain story again!"

"But, Mom, it's true, I swear."

Mom frowned at me. "And I suppose we have to call off the Dairy Dance so the whole town doesn't get wiped out."

"Yeah, exactly. I knew you'd believe me! It's already absorbed Jerry Curdle and Armand and—"

"All right, just stop right there, Billy. We're not going to call off the Dairy Dance. And that's final! I want you to stop making up stories!"

"What's this about calling off the Dairy Dance?" Jonathan Curdle asked. I turned around and saw that he was behind me.

"Oh, nothing, Jonathan. Billy doesn't like it

that I'm spending so much time here instead of staying at home, so he's making up stories."

"Oh, isn't that cute! What kind of stories are you making up now, Billy?"

"The same one he was telling when you were over at the house that first day with Jerry—only now the cheese brain has a name."

"Mom!"

"He calls it Culture 286. According to him, it's already eaten our hired hand and Jerry!"

Jonathan Curdle's eyes went wide for a moment. He started coughing until a thread of drool hung from his shriveled mouth. When he finally stopped coughing, he looked at me and smiled.

"Well, isn't that cute. I guess it's an exciting day for all of us, with the Dairy Dance tonight. The poor little darling is probably just overexcited."

"No, I'm not. You know all about it—and it's your fault!" I cried, pointing at him.

He stopped smiling.

"Isn't that cute—I'm in the story, too," he croaked. "I'm sure I don't know what you're talking about, Billy."

"Oh, yeah? Where's Jerry then?"

"Jerry is—well, he had to leave town to visit his sick cousin. Yes, that's it, he's out of town."

"He had to leave town? What about the Dairy Dance?" Mom asked. "He was supposed to take Jennifer. She's going to be very disappointed."

"Yes, it is a shame, but it can't be helped. Now, Billy, your mother has some work to finish up. Why don't you let me take you down to Nurse Pontiac? You can rest for a while, and your mom can take you home when she's finished."

"That's a good idea," Mom agreed. "You go down and get some rest, and I'll come and get you in about an hour."

Jonathan Curdle reached out a bony hand and clamped it around my arm. "Come with me," he ordered.

"Mom, no, you don't understand!" I cried as Jonathan Curdle dragged me away.

CHAPTER 25

"You can go, Nurse Pontiac. I'll take care of Billy," Mr. Curdle told the huge nurse. She nodded and lumbered out of the room.

Mr. Curdle slammed the door shut and spun around to face me. He had an evil look in his eyes.

"Now then, Billy, why don't you tell me a story," he said gently.

"I don't know any stories."

He walked over to me and rubbed his veiny hands together. He smiled, showing his yellow teeth.

"Oh, I think you do, dear boy. You were telling your mother one—about a certain cheese. We both know where Jerry really is, don't we?"

"Yeah."

"And that is—?"

"He went somewhere to visit his sick cousin,"
I said. "Isn't that what you told Mom?"

He slapped himself in the forehead. His
hands clenched and unclenched like some kind
of weird machine. "Now you listen here, young·
ster! I know all about Culture 286, and you're
going to tell me where it is. Or perhaps you
would like a nice cold glass of milk?"

A glass of milk?

"Oh, yes, I know all about your trouble with
milk, Billy. Your mother told me all about it—a
very sad story indeed. Now, where is Culture
286?"

"I don't know what you're talking about."

He nodded slowly, then went over and
opened the door a crack. "Nurse Pontiac," I
heard him purr. "Would you please get Billy a
nice tall glass of milk? I think it would be good
for him."

Oh, no, not that—he was going to torture
me!

After a few seconds he closed the door and
spun around. He had a big frothy glass of super-
gross milk in his hand. It looked like a big glass
of mucus to me.

He held the milk out toward me. My stomach
started churning. "Now, Billy, would you like to
tell me about Culture 286—or would you like

to toast the Dairy Dance?"

"No way, you old farthead," I cried.

"Farthead? Now really, Billy, is that a polite thing for a little boy to call a nice old man like myself?"

I backed up and stood on the little cot where I was supposed to be resting. He got closer, and my stomach started doing flip-flops. He shoved the milk right in my face.

"Drink it!" he ordered.

Then there was a scream from the outer office. Mr. Curdle glanced at the door and I knocked the glass out of his hand. It shattered on the floor and milk went everywhere. The old man scowled at me and was about to say something when there was another scream and the sounds of a struggle.

"What is going on out there?" he asked. "Has our little friend finally come home?"

The cheese monster—was it at the door?

CHAPTER 26

Bam. Bam. Bam.

The door shook on its hinges and suddenly flew open. I couldn't believe it—it was big and strong and ugly.

It was my sister!

Jennifer rushed into the room and ran to Mr. Curdle. Her hair was in curlers and her face was all red. It looked like one big zit—ready to pop.

"Mr. Curdle, Mr. Curdle!" she screeched. "My mom called and told me Jerry left town. Is that true?" she demanded. "Is it?"

"Calm down now, Jennifer. Yes, it's true. He's gone away for a while, but there will be other boys at the Dairy Dance."

"But I don't want some other boy!" she shouted, pounding on Mr. Curdle's bony chest. "I want Jerry!"

"Just calm down now," he said.

"I can't calm down! I don't have a date for the Dairy Dance!"

That's when I decided to make my exit. Curdle grabbed at me, but I dodged him and ran through the door.

"Just hold on one minute there, young man. Where do you think you're going?" a voice boomed out behind me as a huge hand clamped down on my collar!

"Calm down," Nurse Pontiac said. "I just want to give you a lollipop." She held a sucker out in her right hand.

I could still hear Mr. Curdle trying to deal with Jennifer as I pocketed the lollipop.

"Uh, thanks, Nurse Pontiac," I said.

And then I was out the door.

"So what do we do now?" Fanny asked.

As soon as I escaped from IMP, I called her. She came and met me in front of the Milk Museum.

"Let's put our heads together," I said. "The whole town could be wiped out tonight."

"Yeah, no thanks to you," she said. "I *told* you not to tell your mom. Now Mr. Curdle's on to us."

Just then Fanny pointed at a truck coming up

Main Street. "Hey look, it's Martha!"

Martha was riding in the back of the truck. Then I noticed something that made my blood run cold. On the side of the truck was a sign that read BLEDSOE BUTCHERS—THE BEST IN MEATS FROM HEADS TO FEETS.

"What are they going to do to Martha?" I cried.

Then our station wagon screeched around the corner. Mom and Dad got out of the car.

I ran over to Dad. "What are they going to do to Martha? What's going on?"

Dad chuckled and patted me on the head. "Man does not live by dairy alone. We're roasting her up for the dance tonight!"

CHAPTER 27

"Honey," Mom said, looking at Dad.

"Oh, come on, kiddo, you didn't think I was serious? We're not going to eat her. They're just taking her over to the Barn of Honor at the dance to pretty her up some. That's the vet's truck. He bought it from the butcher yesterday and hasn't had time to paint over the old sign."

Whew! What a relief.

"Now what's this I hear about you running away from Jonathan earlier?" he asked.

"Dad, Mr. Curdle was trying to torture me with a glass of milk. He wants the cheese monster. We have to stop the Dairy Dance before it's too late!"

Dad laughed and wiped his glasses. "That's pretty good, son, but never try to kid a kidder."

"I don't know what's gotten into you, Billy Fudder. But you're coming home, right this minute!" Mom said, grabbing my ear. "You can apologize to Jonathan at the dance tonight."

"But Mom, it's true—we're all in terrible danger!"

"You just get in the car, Billy—right this instant!" She opened the car door and shoved me inside.

I rolled down the window as Dad started up the car. "See you tonight, Fanny. It'll be okay!"

Fanny just shook her head sadly as we drove away. Her cute smile was gone. If we didn't stop that thing, none of us would be smiling any time in the near future!

"I'm not going to the stupid dance!" I heard Jennifer screaming from down the hall. I looked at the White Ninja alarm clock next to my bed. It was six thirty-four—a half hour until zero hour!

Then Dad burst into my room. "It's almost time, son. Are you ready?" He looked kind of funny, because he had put about a pound of gel in his hair to get it to stay down.

Jennifer screamed again and Mom called out, "Yes, you *are* going. Now you unlock the door and come out of the bathroom this instant."

Dad shrugged. "I better go and see what's holding up the womenfolk."

He was picking the lock on the bathroom door with his credit card when I came out of my room.

"Oh, don't you look nice," Mom said.

"Thanks," I told her, pulling at my collar. I was wearing my suit, and my tie was choking me to death.

"There we go!" Dad announced, throwing the bathroom door wide open. Jennifer marched out in her new red ruffled dress and clomped down the stairs.

"All right, I'll go," she said. "But I won't have fun."

If you only knew, I thought.

Everyone in Bledsoe was gathered at the Dairy Dance. A big tent was set up on the lawn in front of the Town Hall. Colorful lights were strung inside the tent. There were bowls of punch—and milk—everywhere. Everything you could possibly make out of milk was there too, on long tables on either side of the tent. Butter in weird shapes, a hundred types of cheese, sour cream, yogurt—it was enough to make a guy totally spew!

"Just keep your eyes open," I told Fanny,

scanning the crowd for trouble. We were standing next to the Barn of Honor. At the end of the tent was the stage, where four guys wearing overalls and red bandannas were playing cheesy fiddle music.

"You look pretty funny in that suit," she said, smiling.

"Well, you look like a dork in that dress!" Actually, I thought she looked kind of pretty in her blue dress with big puffy sleeves. But I wasn't about to tell her.

"Children, children, please, this is no time to be fighting amongst ourselves!" Martha said as she appeared among the small herd in the Barn of Honor. "We must be especially vigilant tonight. The fate of Bledsoe depends on us!"

Suddenly the music stopped.

"Ladies and gentlemen, may I have your attention, please!" It was Mr. Curdle. "Firstly, I would like to thank everyone for being here."

People cheered.

"And secondly, I would like to introduce Ellen Fudder, a new member of our community, who is going to tell us all about the new town slogan."

Curdle hobbled to a seat behind the podium. Mom walked up on stage. She raised her hand for quiet and smiled.

"Well, I'm not much good at public speaking, but here goes—"

Fanny and I were making our way toward the stage when we heard Curdle's voice again. "Not now!" I couldn't see the stage because there were too many people. I looked at Fanny.

"Get that thing out of here!" Curdle shouted.

I jumped up to get a glimpse of the stage. There was something big and white up there. My mom was backing away from it. The crowd got very quiet. I looked over at Fanny, but she was gone—lost in the crowd!

Mr. Curdle screamed. "No, no, no, no!"

CHAPTER
28

I broke through the crowd and raced to the foot of the stage.

"Get that thing out of here," Curdle screeched. "It's not supposed to come onstage until after the presentation."

It was just the cottage cheese sculpture Fanny and I had seen on the back of the truck.

Fanny emerged from the crowd as the workmen wheeled the sculpture backstage. "Maybe we were wrong. Maybe it's not going to show."

"I hope you're right," I said.

Mom smoothed her hair back and took the podium again. The town slogan had changed again to "Everything's Cheesier in Bledsoe."

Fanny rolled her eyes, but I was really proud of Mom.

Everyone clapped, then Mr. Curdle stood up.

"Thank you, Ellen. And now, the moment we've been waiting for—the crowning of Bledsoe's newest Dairy Queen. To do the honors, please welcome Sally Cheddar, the reigning queen."

More applause, then a hefty teenager in a sash and tiara came on stage. She stood next to Mr. Curdle and waved.

I turned to Fanny. "Maybe it'll be you up there someday."

"Give me a break, Milk Dud."

Mr. Curdle tore open an envelope. "And the winner is...Jennifer Fudder!"

I had barely caught my breath from being punched. Now I thought I was going to collapse!

There was pizza-face herself up on the stage. She was blubbering, of course. She looked like a gigantic tomato in her red dress. Sally Cheddar put her crown on Jennifer's head. Then someone wheeled out a big refrigerated case—holding a sculpture of Jennifer's head, carved out of butter!

"Congrats, White Ninja," Fanny said.

I was about to say something when Jonathan Curdle shouted offstage, "No, wait! The sculpture doesn't come out till *after* she makes her speech!"

But it wasn't a sculpture. This time it was Culture 286—heading straight for my sister!

CHAPTER
29

"Jennifer!" I yelled, running for the stage.

People were screaming so loud it hurt.

The cheese stepped forward and took a swipe at my sister. It was dripping with rotten cheese— I wanted to barf! Jonathan Curdle was still standing on the stage, smiling at the creature.

I jumped up on the stage, with Fanny right behind me.

"What *is* that thing?" Jennifer cried.

"I'll explain later. Let's just get out of here!"

Just then a head appeared out of the chest of the cheese. It was Jerry Curdle—and he was all covered with putrid slime!

Jerry screamed as the cheese began to reabsorb him.

"Jerry!" Jennifer yelled, lunging at the cheese.

"Jennifer, don't!" I yelled.

CHAPTER
30

The cheese sucked my sister in. Her brand-new crown clattered to the stage. Rhinestones flew in all directions. Poor Jennifer!

"Jennifer!" Mom and Dad cried at once.

"Billy!" Fanny grabbed me before the cheese could attack again. We ran off the stage. People were still stampeding for the door. "You remember what happened when your barf hit the cheese in the old barn?" she asked.

"Yeah."

"That's what you need to do now," she said. "You have to throw up on it!"

No problem. "I'll just drink some milk," I said.

As I looked at the pitchers of milk and the wheels of cheese on the tables, I could hear Mr. Curdle yelling at the top of his lungs. I picked up a particularly moldy piece of blue cheese and held it up to my nose.

"Yes, my cheese!" Mr. Curdle cried at the top of his lungs. He was standing on the stage face-to-face with the monster. "With you I will rule the world. Nothing can stand in our way!"

The cheese took a step towards him.

"Yes, come to me, my creature! You belong to me!"

The cheese rose up, towering over Mr. Curdle...

CHAPTER
31

He screamed and the cheese fell, covering him completely.

I raised the blue cheese to my lips. It stank. I tried to take a bite—but couldn't!

"C'mon, Billy, hurry up. Bring it over here," Fanny said. "The cheese is blobbing out. Now's our chance!"

I ran over to the stage, where Fanny was standing.

The tent was empty—except for us and Mom and Dad, who kept yelling, "C'mon, kids!"

But I couldn't leave the cheese alive. It was going to be either me or it—there was no other way!

As the cheese re-formed itself, Fanny and I crept up as close to it as we dared.

"Now just take a big bite of cheese," Fanny

said, "and blow chunks all over it!"

I brought the blue cheese to my mouth again. My hands were shaking.

"Man, you picked a super-gross one," Fanny said. "That would even make me spew—and *I* like cheese!"

The cheese monster on the stage quivered some more and began bubbling. Something was happening!

"Eat the cheese!" Fanny screamed.

"I can't eat it. I can't do it!"

"How do you like me now, children?" the cheese monster bellowed suddenly. Now it had Jonathan Curdle's face!

"What do you mean, you can't eat it?" Fanny yelled. "You have to!"

"I can't!"

"Ha, ha!" the new Jonathan Curdle cheese laughed. "With this new body nothing can stop me! Especially not a couple of dorky kids!"

Then I got an idea. "Fanny, burp as if your life depended on it now!"

"Why didn't you just say so?" she shouted.

With his spongy new arms, Cheese Curdle reached down for us...

But we jumped off the stage just in time.

Fanny was swallowing air faster and faster, until—

CHAPTER
32

Buuurrrrrrrraaaaaaaapppppp!

Right in my face! It was the worst one yet. It smelled of rotten eggs and spoiled pork and asparagus and cat boxes and sweaty feet and moldy sour cream and all the freshest, steamiest cow pies in all the pastures of Bledsoe.

Cheese Curdle reached down for us again and I barfed all over his gross arm. Chunky vomit pumped up from my stomach and shot out of my mouth. When it hit him, he screamed. His new body sizzled and smoked.

"Again," I cried. "Do it again, Fanny! It's working!"

She did it again, and—

Deadly chunks all over his legs! Enzyme, do your stuff!

Fanny kept belching and I kept barfing. The

monster crashed to the floor. I hurled on his chest and his back as he writhed in pain. The tent was filled with the smell of vomit and sizzling rotten cheese.

Pretty soon we could see the outline of someone—and Armand appeared! He was covered with vomit and cottage cheese, but still breathing.

My stomach *killed*, but I kept on barfing. All that was left inside me was stomach juices.

Suddenly, another body was ejected from the cheese—Jennifer! She was covered with slime, but she was alive, too.

"Keep going!" Fanny shouted.

I didn't think I could barf anymore, but somehow I did. Finally, when there was almost nothing left of the once-dangerous cheese, Jerry and Jonathan Curdle rolled out.

What a mess!

I fell on the ground, holding my stomach. Mom and Dad rushed over. Mom put her arms around me.

"It's okay, Mom, I'm okay," I told her. I really must have stank.

Dad patted me on the head. "I knew you could do it, son. No cheese is going to get the best of my Billy! I wasn't joking when I told you Bledsoe could be an exciting place once you got used to it."

"You mean you *knew*, Dad? You knew all the time?"

Dad took off his glasses and wiped the slime from them. "Sure, I did. Same thing happened when I was a kid—only then it was sour cream!"

Far off in the distance I could hear sirens blaring. Slowly, people starting coming back into the tent.

"Look!" Fanny said, pointing at what was left of the cheese.

Something was moving. Oh, no, not again!

And then the robin that the cheese had absorbed in the old barn hopped out of the slime. It shook itself off and flew out of the tent.

Then I knew everything was going to be okay!

There's one more

Gooflumps

Don't miss R. U. Slime's other masterpiece!

#2 ½
STAY OUT OF THE
BATHROOM

Another Unauthorized Parody
Not a Goosebumps Book